MEN IN LOVE

OPEN TO *Possibilities*

CAROL LYNNE

ELLORA'S CAVE
ROMANTICA®
WWW.ELLORASCAVE.COM

An Ellora's Cave Publication

www.ellorascave.com

Open to Possibilities

ISBN 9781419964275

Edited by Helen Woodall.
Cover artist Syneca.

Electronic book publication September 2007
Trade paperback publication 2011

OPEN TO POSSIBILITIES

&

Dedication

ꟸ

To my cousins and my sisters. Thank you for believing in me.

Author Note

ꟸ

The author freely acknowledges the United States' "don't ask, don't tell" policy in the U.S. Military, but in her world, all men are created equal.

Trademarks Acknowledgement

ꟸ

The author acknowledges the trademarked status and trademark owners of the following wordmarks mentioned in this work of fiction:

Big Mac: McDonald's Corporation

Stetson: John B. Stetson Company

Chapter One

ꟸ

Riding across his dry west Oklahoma land, Gabe Whitlock ran his eyes over the pastures. Dry. Everywhere he looked the water had dried up. He pulled back on the reins, gently stopping his buckskin mare Lolly, and dismounted. He led Lolly over to the dry creek bed and took off his battered straw Stetson. "Damn, Lolly, there isn't even enough water here for you, let alone four hundred head of cattle."

He mounted his horse again and rode toward the barn to find Rex Cotton. Gabe bought the ranch a month ago and Rex Cotton was his foreman. Although Cotton knew a lot more about cattle than Gabe did, he was always willing to teach Gabe what he needed to know.

Gabe's old friend Jake Baker's father used to own the ranch but Jake sold it to him when his father was killed. The one stipulation of the sale was that Rex Cotton received total ownership of his foreman's house and he had a job as foreman as long as he was physically able.

The main problem aside from the lack of water on the Double B was the main ranch house. Gabe just couldn't get a good night's sleep in it. Buck Baker, Jake's father, had raped and branded his stepdaughter in the upstairs bedroom when she was just eighteen. Seven years later Buck tracked Jenny down again and kidnapped her from the hospital after he shot her and brought her here to the Double B and held her in the basement. Jake was married to Jenny now as well as to Cree Sommers. It was an odd arrangement to most folks but it worked well for the three of them.

The problem was the house. Every time Gabe was in the house he felt dirty. He had no idea when he'd bought the place that he'd feel that way in his own home but he did. Gabe hadn't had a good night's sleep in a month.

He took his hat off again as he rode toward the barn and ran his fingers through his short dark brown hair. He needed to find Cotton. They would have to figure out what to do about the water or his cattle would die of thirst. Thinking of Cotton made Gabe's jeans feel a size too small in the crotch. That was one handsome man.

Jake had talked about Cotton several times but he pictured an old man with snow white hair. Although Cotton was older, forty-six to Gabe's thirty-two, he was by no means an old man. His hair had once been black as night but was liberally peppered with gray now, at least in front. It gave him a distinguished appearance, Gabe thought. Cotton was about six foot three, the same height as he was, but where Gabe was built like a brick outhouse Cotton was lean and sinewy. Cotton had the body of someone much younger. Gabe loved the way his legs seemed to go on forever and the veins in his arms bulged. That, more than the size of his biceps, signaled the amount of muscle in his lean frame.

Gabe pulled up to the barn and dismounted. He led Lolly over to the water trough and tied her to the fence. He went into the barn and grabbed his grooming supplies. Gabe yelled for Cotton but received no answer. He went back to Lolly and took off her saddle and blanket. He was brushing her down when Cotton spoke behind him.

"Did I hear you calling my name?" He walked closer and lifted the saddle and blanket off the fence.

"Yeah. I wanted to talk to you about the lack of water for the cattle but it can wait if you're busy." Gabe continued to brush Lolly down, trying his best not to look at Cotton.

"No, I'm not busy. Just let me put these away for you and I'll grab a couple beers from the fridge and meet you on my porch." Cotton carried the saddle and blanket into the barn.

Gabe finished grooming Lolly and released her into the pasture with a flake of hay. He made his way to Cotton's two-bedroom log home. It had a nice deep front porch with a couple of rocking chairs, perfect for sitting after a long hot day.

Gabe climbed the five steps leading up to the porch and sat in the rocker beside Cotton. Cotton handed him a cold beer and he took a long pull. "Damn, that hits the spot. There's nothing like a cold beer to quench your thirst." Gabe took off his hat and sat it on his knee. He rifled his hand through his sweaty hair trying to get rid of his "hat hair".

Cotton was staring at him when he looked over. Cotton quickly looked away and took a drink. "You're right about that, Gabe. Beer is the nectar of the gods." He finished his beer and got up. "I'm ready for another, what about you?"

Gabe quickly drank the rest of his beer and held out the bottle. "I could drink another one." Cotton reached for the bottle and their fingers brushed against each other. Gabe felt like a bolt of lightning was traveling down his arm straight to his cock.

Cotton looked at him for a minute and went inside. He came back a few minutes later and handed Gabe another beer, being careful not to touch him again. Cotton took his seat and turned toward Gabe. "I've been thinking about our water problem and the way I see it we have two choices. We can haul water in for the cattle or we can sell 'em. I think we should compromise and sell some of the cattle and still haul water. Maybe if you could afford to sell off enough cattle we could divide what's left between the east and south pastures. The windmill in the east pasture is still drawing enough to water about a hundred head of cattle and the south pasture windmill could water another seventy-five or so.

"We could always haul water in for the rest but it would mean hauling water all day from town. If you figure in the man-hours and the price of gas to do that I don't know that you'd come out ahead." Cotton took his hat off and ran his hands through his thick silvery black hair.

Gabe was mesmerized by the sight of Cotton's long, thin fingers running through that thick gorgeous hair. He realized Cotton was looking at him for some sort of answer. "I'll have to go over the books again and check the internet for current cattle prices but I'm sure I can sell at least part of the herd." Gabe sat his empty bottle on the porch and yawned. He covered his mouth as he yawned a second time. "Sorry about that. I haven't been sleeping well."

Cotton finished off his beer and set the empty bottle down also. "What's keeping you awake? I hope it's not the water situation because that's just part of ranching in western Oklahoma. You'll get used to it."

Gabe yawned again and shook his head. "No, it's not the water, it's that damn house. I haven't had a good night's sleep since I moved in. I can't help but to feel dirty every time I think about what Buck did inside that house. If I had the money I'd bulldoze the damn thing down and start from scratch."

Cotton looked over and nodded. "I understand what you're saying. I can't even stand to go into the kitchen over there, let alone trying to sleep in the bedroom. Why don't you gather some of your things and move into my spare bedroom? You can figure out what to do about the house later. Right now you need to get some sleep before you fall over. I was also going to talk to you about renaming the ranch. You own it now, it should be a name you choose."

Gabe stretched his arms over his head. "I think I'll take you up on that spare room for a while. At least until I figure out what to do about the house. I'm not sure about changing the name of the ranch. How would that work exactly? I mean, the cattle have all been branded with the Double B brand. Would we have to re-brand them?"

"No, we can just register the brand change with the state. They'll have all the information on file when it comes time to sell the cattle." Cotton stood and picked up his and Gabe's empty bottles. "Why don't you think of the name change while you pack up some of your things? I'll go put fresh sheets on the bed and empty out the closet."

Gabe nodded and headed toward the main house. He couldn't believe what he was doing. How would he be able to live with a man he lusted after every day and stay away from him? Gabe shook his head, he didn't know but he had to do something. His body was wearing down fast with no sleep. He'd just have to think of Cotton as his foreman and friend not as the sexy-as-sin cowboy in the next room.

* * * * *

Rex was kicking himself as he changed the sheets on the double bed. What else could he have done? Gabe was obviously exhausted. Rex couldn't imagine trying to sleep in that house. Hell, he even hated to look at it. The problem was he liked to look at its owner. He'd had his eye on Gabe since the first time he'd seen him. Gabe came to the ranch with the rest of his ex-SEAL team to help rescue Jenny from Buck.

Rex noticed Gabe right away. He was tall and broad, tapering down to the hardest, sexiest ass he'd ever seen. His hair had been cut military short but the dark brown strands were starting to grow out now. His longer hair framed his light gray eyes to perfection.

Rex remembered watching him stretch on the porch a few minutes ago. He thought Gabe's white t-shirt was going to rip at the seams as his muscles flexed. Rex was getting hard just thinking about it.

He finished making the bed and went to the closet. Not much was really stored in here—some old Christmas decorations and winter clothes. Rex decided he'd box up the clothes and take them to the main house for storage. He pulled out the big box of Christmas stuff and carried it to the porch. Then he went to the supply shed to look for a couple of empty boxes for his clothes. He found what he was looking for and headed back to his house.

Rex boxed up the clothes and set them on the porch. He decided it would be easier to just haul the boxes in his truck to the main house. That way Gabe could use it to haul his stuff too. He pulled his cherry red quad-cab pickup up to the porch and loaded the three boxes.

He drove the short distance to the main house and began unloading. Once he got all the boxes on the porch, he let himself in the front door. He would just take them up to Jake's old bedroom. Rex knew Gabe wasn't using it for anything. He carried the first box up the stairs and stopped. He heard a grunting noise coming from Gabe's bedroom. Thinking Gabe might need some help lifting something, Rex opened the door.

Gabe was stretched out on the bed with his jeans down to his knees and his shaft in his hand. He was so busy working his cock he didn't hear Rex open the door. Rex knew he should leave and shut the door but his feet were glued to the floor and his eyes were glued to the huge dark red cock in Gabe's fist. Gabe started really pumping his cock and reached back to finger his own asshole. It was the most erotic thing Rex had ever seen. Rex knew Gabe was about to come so he stepped out and quietly shut the door. Just when the door was almost shut Gabe must have started coming because he moaned and groaned and then he called out a name. Rex shut the door and closed his eyes. Fuck him. Gabe had just called out Cotton's name as he came. Rex didn't have time to think about it now.

He quietly crept back down the stairs and out the front door. He stood in front of the door again and knocked loudly and then opened the door and called Gabe's name. "Gabe! I thought it might be okay if I stored a few boxes in Jake's old room." He started climbing the stairs and came face-to-face with Gabe at the top. "Oh hi. I thought I'd store a couple boxes in Jake's room if that sounds all right."

Gabe nodded and shifted from foot to foot. "Yeah. That's fine. No reason not to use the house for something."

Rex carried the box into Jake's room and put it in the closet. "I brought my pickup so we can haul your stuff down to my place."

Gabe nodded and went into his room. Rex followed him. He noticed Gabe's scent as soon as he entered the small bedroom. Gabe's cologne smelled like citrus fruit but the room was a combination of his cologne and his seed. The combination was overwhelming to Rex's senses. He grabbed a suitcase and headed out of the room. "I'll just take this down while I'm at it."

Gabe stopped packing another suitcase and looked up. "Oh, okay. Thanks, Cotton."

Rex continued loading the truck until all of Gabe's things were in the back. "Is that all?"

Nodding his head, Gabe climbed into the four-wheel drive and shut the door. When Rex climbed in Gabe turned to him sheepishly. "I know it's sad for a man my age but I don't have many material possessions. I guess it comes from a childhood spent moving from one foster home to another. You learn really quickly to travel light, otherwise the things you get attached to get left behind." Gabe looked out the side window.

Rex felt a knot form in his stomach. He could see that Gabe still carried around a lot of pain from his childhood. "Is that where you learned to ride so well? I mean, were some of the foster homes ranches?"

Gabe nodded. Rex thought that was all he was going to get out of him but he cleared his throat and began speaking in a soft faraway voice.

"The foster homes were in and around Cheyenne, Wyoming. Most folks that took me in just seemed to want an extra ranch hand. It was perfect for them. They got help with the chores and someone actually paid them for it. After the busy season was over I always got sent away to a new home. It was a cycle. I'd spend my summers on ranches and my winters usually in town with a family that had a houseful of foster kids." Gabe shrugged his shoulders. "At least I learned a lot about horses. They became my only friends. I didn't have a single friend until I joined the Navy and entered the SEAL unit. Those five guys that made up my team—Remy, Ben, Nicco, Jake and Cree—became the only family I've ever had."

Rex pulled the truck up to his porch and sat there. He wanted to pull Gabe into his arms and comfort the sad lonely little boy inside him. Instead he reached his arm across the cab and put it on Gabe's shoulder. "You've got a home of your own now, Gabe."

Gabe wiped his eyes and turned to face Cotton. "Yeah. A home I'm too freaked out to even sleep in." He got out of the truck and went to unload his stuff.

Rex joined him at the tailgate. "Consider my house your home. I want you to be comfortable here, Gabe." He picked up the two suitcases and headed to the spare bedroom.

Gabe followed, carrying a box of books and miscellaneous stuff. He set the box on the bed next to the suitcases. "Thanks for this, Cotton."

Nodding, Rex started to leave the room. "I'm going to put a chicken in the oven for dinner then go out to the barn and work until suppertime. You unpack and make yourself at home."

Cotton left and Gabe sat down on the bed and put his head in his hands. How was he going to do this? Already the feelings he was experiencing had caused him to jack off in his old bedroom. How many times a day would he have to do it living in the same house with Cotton?

He got up and opened the first suitcase. He opened the nearby dresser drawer and started putting his socks, t-shirts and sweats away. Gabe didn't wear underwear so that was one less thing to put away. He emptied the first suitcase and opened the second. He hauled out the jeans and put them in the bottom two drawers. He only had a couple of nice dress-type clothes. He hung up his only suit and a few dress shirts along with a pair of khaki pants. He took the empty suitcases and pushed them under the bed. The box was easy to unpack—it was mostly books. Gabe lined them up on a nearby empty shelf and pulled out the only picture he had. It was a picture of his SEAL team in front of a bar in South America. He put the picture on top of his dresser. His alarm clock went beside his bed and the shaving kit he took to the bathroom.

After he was done unpacking everything he owned, he wandered through the house. Well, that wasn't exactly true. Technically he owned this ranch but that fact still hadn't completely sunk in. To a man who'd never had ties to anything, having a place to call home felt alien. He looked around the living room, seeing it in detail for the first time. Cotton had decorated the log home in an old cowboy kind of way. He had antique tools and horseshoes displayed on the walls in the living room. A painting of a pasture full of cattle with a lone rider sat over his river-rock fireplace. He noticed Cotton didn't have any chairs in here, only two couches facing each other on either side of the fireplace. Of course the couches were leather to go along with the cowboy rustic theme.

Gabe looked at the pictures on the bookcase in the corner of the room. Pictures of Cotton on the ranch working and a couple of him with an older woman, who must be his mother because she had the same black hair Cotton did. Gabe wondered if Cotton's mother was still alive. Hell, he wondered if his own mother was still alive. He'd never known her but he knew she existed somewhere. He shook off the thought and went through the doorway to the kitchen.

The kitchen was done in the same style as the rest of the house but in here Cotton had hung old cooking utensils on the walls. The cabinets were painted a sage green with a walnut countertop. Gabe ran his hand over the smooth-looking wood. A small sage green painted table and four chairs sat in the breakfast nook. Overall the house was fairly small but very nice. It felt like…a home. Tears started to burn the back of Gabe's eyes.

He physically shook his head and went out to the porch. He was an ex-SEAL, for Christ's sake. Where was all this emotion coming from? He was supposed to be tough. Hell, he was tough but something about being in Cotton's house tightened his chest. He headed to the barn to see if he could help Cotton. He'd noticed on the way through the kitchen that the timer on the oven said the chicken had another fifty minutes. Might as well make himself useful in the meantime.

He entered the barn and looked around for Cotton. He saw him leaning on his buckskin gelding Chief's stall. Gabe started walking toward him. "Hey, Cotton, can I help you with anything before dinner?"

Startled, Cotton spun around, cock in hand. He quickly turned back around and tried to stuff himself back into his jeans. Gabe's mouth went dry and then began to water at the sight of Cotton's plum-colored cock. Next to his friend Ben's cock Cotton's was the biggest he'd ever seen.

Cotton faced him once more and put his hat back on. "Sorry about that, Gabe." Cotton picked up the grain bucket and emptied it into Chief's grain bin.

Gabe was still thinking about Cotton's cock. Cotton must have picked up on where Gabe's thoughts were because the next thing Gabe knew Cotton had dropped the bucket and was standing toe to toe with him.

Cotton leaned closer to Gabe and whispered, "I want you, Gabe." A mere second later his lips came crashing down on Gabe's. Gabe wrapped his arms around Cotton and pulled him in closer.

Rubbing his own hard cock against Cotton's, he thrust his tongue into his mouth. The kiss had absolutely no finesse to it. It was all raw, hungry need. Cotton didn't seem to mind. He was breathing just as hard as Gabe was. Gabe broke the kiss and licked the side of Cotton's face. "Feels so good…want you."

Cotton reached down and unbuttoned Gabe's jeans and pulled out Gabe's rock-hard cock and started stroking it. "God, you feel good."

Gabe returned the favor and unzipped Cotton and pushed down his boxer briefs. Cotton's still rock-hard erection sprang up into Gabe's waiting hand. He felt the veins bulging along the side of the thick long cock and began to pump. Gabe thrust his hips into Cotton's hand. "Not gonna last, Cotton."

Cotton continued the assault on his mouth and cock. "Come for me." He ran his hand over the top of Gabe's cock and fingered the slit on top.

Gabe came, yelling Cotton's name, splashing his seed all over Cotton's fist. Cotton came a split second later, howling up to the rafters. Gabe kissed Cotton again and reached into his back pocket for a handkerchief. He brought Cotton's hand up off his still semi-hard cock and wiped it clean. He then cleaned his own hands and stuffed the cloth back into his pocket.

Cotton wrapped his arms around Gabe and leaned in until they were forehead to forehead. "Please call me Rex. Cotton is my foreman name and right now I just want to be the man that I am." He ran his long fingers through Gabe's hair and kissed him again. This time a little slower, adding in the finesse that was lacking before.

Gabe broke the kiss and looked into Cot—Rex's eyes. "Is this really happening?"

Rex looked down at both their cocks and smiled. "I hope so, Gabe. I've wanted you since you showed up to rescue Jenny from Buck. I even went and had a test run in case anything should happen between the two of us. When I walked into the main house earlier and saw you on the bed with your cock in your hand…" Rex took a deep breath. "Damn. I knew it would happen eventually but what sealed it for me was you calling my name as you came. It was the sexiest damn thing I've ever witnessed."

Gabe ran his tongue around the rim of Rex's lips. "I'm clean too. I don't have the paperwork to verify it but I've never in my life done anything without a condom. The last time I was intimate with anyone was three years ago right after I got out of the Navy."

Rex pulled away to look into Gabe's eyes. "I believe you, Gabe, but why three years? It seems like a long time between encounters."

Gabe shrugged and pulled his pants back up and buttoned them. "I was tired of sex with no feeling. It just wasn't enough anymore. So I decided just to wait until I found someone I could really enjoy being with in and out of bed."

Rex zipped up his own jeans. He looked into Gabe's beautiful gray eyes. "Thank you for choosing me. I feel the same way about you." Rex broke the eye contact and looked around the barn. "Although I could have thought of a better place than the barn for our first encounter. The important thing is that we both took the chance. Let's finish up in here. I'm sure the chicken is almost done and I want to pop a couple of potatoes in the microwave."

Chapter Two

ꟃ

They finished bedding the horses down for the night and went inside. Rex finished dinner as Gabe brought his laptop to the kitchen table and started going over the books. "I think if we cut back on a few things we'll be able to sell off a good portion of the cattle and still be in the black for the year. Depending on how the wells hold up, that is."

Rex put the food on the table and Gabe shut down the computer. "I'll get the drinks." Gabe opened the refrigerator and looked inside. "Do you want lemonade or tea?"

Rex put a plate of bread on the table and turned to Gabe. "Tea, please. I always have tea with meals and lemonade on the porch in the evening." He smiled a crooked sideways smile. "If I'm not having a beer, that is." Rex walked over to Gabe and took the glass of tea from him. He leaned in close and kissed him. "What do you want to do after dinner?"

Gabe smiled and took his own glass of tea to the table and sat down. "I think you know what I have in mind but first we both need to take a shower." Gabe looked down at the semen stains on his shirt and jeans. "And we need to change our clothes…or just take them off for the evening." He waggled his eyebrows at Rex.

Rex laughed and sat down at the table. "Okay, dinner…shower…bed…talk and then some much-needed sleep for you. I hope I can talk you into sharing my bed tonight?"

Gabe looked at him. "Just try keeping me out of it after what happened in the barn. I learned a few tricks in the SEALs."

They filled their plates and ate dinner while talking lightly. After dinner Gabe helped Rex clean the kitchen and put the leftovers in the fridge with a few quick gropes thrown in. When the kitchen was clean Rex pulled Gabe toward the bathroom. "Let's get you clean, sweetheart."

Gabe stopped Rex's forward progress and pulled him up against his chest. "No one's ever called me by an actual endearment before."

Rex could see the pain on Gabe's face as he said the words. "Does it bother you? If it does, just tell me and I'll stop. It just came out of my mouth naturally."

Gabe kissed him and shook his head. "No, I like it. I'm just afraid I'll start depending on it."

Rex wrapped his arms tighter around the big, muscled man in front of him. "You can depend on me, sweetheart. I've no plans to ever leave this ranch." He kissed him, opening his mouth and delving his tongue into the moist recesses of Gabe's mouth. He broke the kiss and pulled Gabe into the bathroom.

The bathroom was the one thing he'd splurged on when Buck built him this house. Rex put his own money into the bathroom so he could have what he'd always dreamed of. A giant picture window sat over the large garden tub and he had a separate walk-in shower. The tile was cobalt blue and white. Rex was glad he'd spent the money now. He turned on the multi-head shower and got out some towels and draped them over the towel warmer on the wall.

Gabe started taking off his clothes and turned toward the sink and dug his toothbrush out of his shaving kit. "I'm going to brush before we shower. Would you like me to shave as well?"

Rex shook his head. "I like the rough feel of your whiskers on my skin. But I will join you and brush my own teeth." Rex took his toothbrush out of the holder and started brushing alongside Gabe. When he was finished he motioned to the holder. "You can put your toothbrush in with mine and your shaving stuff in the drawer if you want."

"Thanks. That would be great." Gabe put his stuff away, suddenly feeling a little awkward. He turned to get in the shower and found Rex already in it. He was soaping his hair and Gabe couldn't help notice the way the bubbles from the shampoo ran down his lean muscled chest. Gabe licked his lips as his gaze lowered to the filling cock jutting out from Rex's body. Gabe knew he had to have a taste of that cock.

He walked into the shower stall and closed the glass door. Immediately he knelt in front of Rex and swallowed his cock all the way to the base. Rex reached down and grabbed the back of his head and thrust his cock even farther down Gabe's throat. They both began a quick rhythm and when Gabe reached behind Rex to finger his hole, Rex grunted and shot down his throat. Gabe licked him clean and stood to kiss him, sharing the taste of Rex's seed.

Rex pulled out of the kiss to take a breath. "Damn, sweetheart, you're the first person to ever take all of me down your throat." Rex kissed him again. "It must mean we're meant to be together."

Gabe kissed him back and nodded. "You're the first person to ever come down my throat. I'm a total virgin when it comes to no-condom sex. By the way, I love the taste of you."

Rex kissed him again and knelt before Gabe. "My turn now, sweetheart." Gabe spread his legs a little farther apart and leaned back against the shower wall. Rex wrapped his fist around Gabe's impressive erection and tongued his sac. He took the balls one by one into his mouth gently sucking and kneading them. Rex ran his tongue back a little farther to the small divot just behind Gabe's balls.

Gabe groaned and thrust his hips toward Rex's mouth. "Ohhhh…suck me, baby…suck my cock."

Rex ran his tongue up the side of Gabe's cock and over the ridge of the head. He swirled his tongue around the head and tongued the slit. Gabe groaned again. Rex looked up into Gabe's face and opened his mouth and swallowed him all the way to the back of his throat.

Rex started a low vibrating hum in the back of his throat and Gabe struggled to hang on. "Gonna come, baby." Rex began swallowing, using his throat muscles to milk Gabe's cock. Gabe thrust as deeply as he could and sent his seed down Rex's throat. He started to sag down the shower wall and Rex stood and held him up in a tight embrace.

He kissed him and reached for the shampoo. "Time to get cleaned up. I think the hot water is about to run out." He shampooed Gabe's hair and washed the rest of his body, paying particular attention to Gabe's asshole.

"Mmm…that feels great, baby. Let's get out and go to bed. I wanna hold you." Gabe turned and shut off the shower.

Rex stepped out first and retrieved the warm bath towels. "Here, this will feel like heaven against your skin." He handed one of the towels to Gabe.

Gabe took the towel and started drying off. "The towel feels great but you feel like heaven to me." He smiled and winked at Rex.

They made their way into the bedroom. Rex's bedroom was done in shades of blue and gray. The predominant piece of furniture in the room was the high California king-size bed. The head and footboard were made of willow branches woven together. Gabe pulled back the covers and jumped into bed. He stretched out on the huge bed. "Great bed, baby. Now I know you won't get me out of it. I could fall asleep right now and not wake up for three days."

Rex crawled in beside him and pulled him into his arms. "Talk first, remember. Then you can sleep. I want to know more about you. What your favorite color is, your favorite food, that kind of stuff?"

Gabe rubbed his cheek against Rex's chest. "Well, let's see…my favorite color is green. Dark green like your eyes. My favorite food would have to be anything Mexican and I like country music. Now it's your turn."

Rex kissed the top of Gabe's head and ran his hand up and down his back. "I'd say blue would have to be my favorite color although suddenly I like gray more and more." He looked down into Gabe's pale gray eyes. "I've got a major sweet tooth so my favorite food would be any kind of dessert and I also like country music."

Gabe ran his fingers around Rex's nipples, watching the tiny nubs grow and become stiff. He leaned over and licked one and then the other. "I saw a couple of pictures in the living room of you and an older woman. Is she your mom?"

Rex could feel his cock already starting to get hard again but this discussion was too important to put off. He needed to know more about Gabe's past. "Yeah, that's my mom, Maggie. She's in a nursing home now over in Styler. I hate that she's there but she's had a stroke since those pictures were taken. She's in a wheelchair now and I didn't have much choice. The ranch isn't exactly set up for wheelchair access."

Gabe licked his nipple again and took the nub into his mouth for a short suckle. "What about your dad?"

Rex involuntarily thrust his hips at the sensation of Gabe's mouth on him. "He died when I was a teenager. He was half-Indian and an alcoholic. He died in a bar fight just before I turned fifteen." He kissed the top of Gabe's head again and ran his hand down the white globe of Gabe's rock-hard ass. "What about you, sweetheart? Do you know anything about your family?"

Gabe rubbed his cheek on the side of Rex's neck and kissed his jaw. "I don't remember my mother much. She left me sitting on a bench in front of a drugstore in Cheyenne when I was about three. I don't know why but she must have had her reasons. I don't even know who my father is. An employee at the drugstore found me when she went to lock up for the night. She took me to the police station and I was put into foster care. I was shuffled from home to home until I turned eighteen and joined the Navy."

Rex's jaw tightened and he tried to swallow around the lump that had formed in his throat. "No one ever abused you, did they, sweetheart?"

Gabe wiped a drop of moisture off his cheek and shook his head. "Abused? No. Loved? No."

Rex couldn't talk after that. He wrapped his arms tighter around Gabe and scooted down level with his face. He ran his hand down the side of Gabe's face and looked deep into his sad eyes. "I think I could. Love you, that is. If you'll give me the chance."

Gabe's eyes filled with tears and he tried to look away. "I'm not really sure if I'm worthy. I mean, if my own mother can't love me enough not to abandon me, how can I expect anyone else to?"

Rex kissed him. "Oh sweetheart. First of all, you don't know why your mother left you. She could have been mentally ill or homeless. Maybe she loved you so much she knew you'd be better away from her. Secondly, I believe you're very worthy of my love and since in this bed you're not the boss of me I can love you if I want to." Rex smiled to try to lighten the mood. "For now just let me hold you while you sleep. I'll still be here when you wake up."

Gabe just nodded and rested his head in the crook of Rex's neck. "Thank you, baby."

Chapter Three

ꩠ

Rex woke the next morning with his chest pressed against Gabe's back. He could feel his morning wood pressing against the crack of Gabe's ass. He kissed Gabe's neck and started sliding his swollen cock up and down Gabe's warm crevice. When Gabe started pushed back into him he knew he was awake.

Gabe reached around behind him and pulled Rex's butt closer still. Rex stopped rubbing and started thrusting. "I want this ass, sweetheart. I want to fuck you so deep you'll never forget me."

"Mmm…yeah, baby, do it." Gabe turned around onto his back.

Rex grabbed a bottle of lubricant out of the bedside drawer and knelt between Gabe's spread thighs. He bent over and took Gabe's cock into his mouth for a quick suck. Gabe moaned and spread his thighs even farther apart. He hooked his arms underneath his knees and presented his hole to Rex.

"Damn, that's a pretty sight." Rex squeezed some lube onto his fingers and began preparing the puckered hole in front of him. He tested Gabe's hole by putting first one and then two fingers deep into his channel. Gabe pushed back into his fingers.

When Rex found the small gland he was looking for and pressed, Gabe almost jumped off the bed. "Fuck, that feels great. I need your cock inside me, baby."

Rex pulled his fingers out and lubed up his cock. He knew it had been awhile for Gabe and he didn't want to hurt him. He lined up his cock and slowly pushed it past the ring of muscles. It was taking all of his control to go slowly. Gabe's ass was so hot and tight, Rex thought he might come before he even got his cock all the way in. "God, you're so tight, sweetheart. You feel so fucking fantastic."

Gabe thrust his ass up into Rex's cock. "Fuck me harder. I won't break."

That was all the invitation Rex needed. He slammed his cock as hard as he could into Gabe's ass. He gave them both just a second to acclimatize then Rex began thrusting in and out of Gabe's tight hole.

Gabe grabbed his own cock and started jerking. "Not gonna last, baby." Gabe grunted and groaned in time to the slams in his ass.

Sweat was dripping off Rex's face by the time Gabe's cock erupted. Rex knew that was his cue to let himself go. He slammed in three more times and blasted his cum deep into the recesses of Gabe's ass. Rex collapsed on top of Gabe, totally spent and sated. "Can we wake up like this every morning?"

Gabe laughed and smacked Rex's ass. "Up and at 'em, cowboy. We've got cattle to sell today."

Rex groaned and rolled off Gabe. "You should really be nicer to your elders."

Gabe flashed his teeth and waggled his brows. "Anyone who can fuck me the way you just did is in no way going to be considered an elder by me."

Rex got up and stopped Gabe as he started for the bathroom. "Does it bother you at all that I'm so much older?"

Gabe pulled him into his arms. "I wouldn't consider fourteen years a huge age gap, but the fact is I like the way you look. I like that your hair is going gray and I even like the tiny lines around your eyes. It doesn't hurt that you still have the hard body of a man in his twenties."

Rex nodded and kissed him. "Okay, I just wanted to make sure. Although you know I'll always be fourteen years older than you. Are you prepared for a senior citizen in your bed when you're still in your prime?"

Smiling, Gabe bit Rex's lower lip then soothed the hurt with his tongue. "As long as you're in my bed I don't care how old you get."

"Good. That's what I wanted to hear. Now get in the shower while I start breakfast." Rex took the opportunity to slap Gabe on his ass this time.

Rex went into the kitchen and made a pot of coffee. He reached into the fridge and took out some bacon and sausage. He put the meat on the stove to fry and started mixing up a batch of biscuits. He popped the biscuits in the oven and went out to the henhouse to gather the eggs. Rex didn't keep many chickens anymore, only eight, including the rooster. He was back in the house before the rest of the breakfast was done. He set the seven eggs in the sink and gently washed the shells. He looked over and saw the coffee was finally done. Rex got out two cups and filled them. He was setting them on the table when Gabe came in. "Perfect timing. Just watch the meat and put it on the platter in a few minutes and when the timer goes off pull the biscuits out of the oven. I'm going to take a quick shower."

Gabe shook his head. "I can't believe you've been cooking breakfast naked. What if you'd burned your important parts?"

Rex laughed and slapped him on the back. "Hell, that's the least of it. I went out to the henhouse and gathered the morning eggs."

Gabe doubled over laughing. "You're damn lucky that big rooster you've got out there didn't go for your worm."

"Worm, hell," Rex stroked the length of his cock. "This is no worm, or couldn't you tell when it was fucking that fine ass of yours?" Rex put his nose in the air and went to take a shower.

By the time Rex got back from his shower breakfast was on the table. He stopped by Gabe's chair and gave him a quick kiss. "Smells good, sweetheart," he said, getting another cup of coffee. "So who do you want me to call about the cattle?"

Setting his coffee cup down, Gabe ran his fingers through his hair. "Well, I was just thinkin' about that. I've decided to call Jake and see if he'd be interested in any of them and then maybe Ben. After that I guess you know more people around here that might buy some."

"That sounds like a good plan. I think you should keep all seven bulls and sell about two hundred of the rest. Maybe about seventy-five of the young steers we should keep. If we can get them plenty of water and grass or hay they should fatten up nicely and the bulls we can always sell if times get tough." Rex finished his breakfast and pushed his plate away. "I'll take care of the dishes while you put a call in to Jake." Rex got up and started clearing the table.

Gabe reached over and grabbed the phone off the wall. He dialed Jake's number and watched Rex move gracefully about the kitchen while he waited for someone to answer.

"Triple Spur."

"Hey, Jake, how's it goin'?" Gabe continued to watch Rex as his cock started to harden in his jeans. Gabe spread his legs wider to give himself more room.

"Hi, Gabe. It's going good here. Jenny's getting nice and big. We can actually feel the babies move now. How is everything on the Double B?"

"Well, that's the main reason I'm calling. It's been so dry here this summer that all my ponds and creeks have gone dry. I'm going to have to sell off about two hundred head and was wondering if you're in the market for any cattle?" Gabe couldn't take it anymore and unsnapped his fly. His angry red cock sprang into his hand. He watched Rex's ass while he did the dishes and slowly stroked himself.

"Well, I'd have to ask my foreman how many head we have room for but I'm definitely interested. Buck always did have some damn fine cattle… Damn it, Cree, I can't think with your mouth wrapped around my cock. Sorry about that, Gabe. Cree seems to think my cock is fair game as soon as I get on the damn phone. Not that I usually mind but I can't very well conduct a business transaction when he's suckin' me off."

Gabe chuckled, which brought Rex's head around. Rex raised one eyebrow and sauntered toward him. Gabe held up his hand, stalling him for a minute. "Well, why don't you talk to your foreman and get back to me. Do you think Ben would be interested in any of them?"

"Um... Mmmm...I'll ask and call you back in a couple hours. Bye, Gabe."

Gabe smiled and hung up the phone. He looked at Rex standing in front of him with his jeans unzipped and his cock and sac hanging out. "Damn, you're sexy. Come closer and let me have a taste of that big python." Gabe hoped that comment would nullify the worm comment he made earlier.

Rex took two more steps and painted Gabe's lips with pre-cum. He leaned in farther and Gabe took his cock into his mouth. Rex put one hand on the table and the other on Gabe's shoulder. As Gabe was sucking his cock Rex toed off his boots and pushed down his jeans and underwear. Rex repositioned his legs and straddled Gabe's lap. "Fuck me, Gabe."

Gabe pulled off Rex's cock and looked up into his eyes. "Pass me the butter."

Rex reached over and pulled the butter dish closer to Gabe. Gabe dipped three fingers into the butter dish and scooped out a decent amount. He wasted no time in lubing Rex's ass. He slicked down his own cock and held it stable while Rex slowly lowered himself onto Gabe's shaft. "Oh fuck, you feel good, baby."

As Rex lowered himself onto Gabe's cock, he was glad for his long legs. He rested his feet on the floor which gave him the leverage to move himself up and down easily on Gabe's dick. "Fill me so good, sweetheart."

Gabe held on to Rex's hips and helped him move up and down on his lap. Gabe started thrusting upward to meet Rex's hungry hole. Rex started moving faster and Gabe's balls began to draw up tightly. "Gonna come in your ass, baby."

Rex threw his head back and erupted all over Gabe's clean shirt. Gabe saw Rex spurt and came deep in his ass. Rex collapsed, resting his head on the top of Gabe's. "Damn, that was good, sweetheart."

Gabe kissed Rex's jaw. "Damn good. Although now I have to go change my t-shirt again."

Rex looked down at the cum-stained black t-shirt. "You'd better throw that in the wash before it dries." He started laughing and untangled himself from Gabe. Rex went over to a kitchen drawer and pulled out a dishcloth. He ran it under warm water and took it back over to clean Gabe up. When he was finished with Gabe he rinsed the cloth out and cleaned himself. Pulling up his jeans and underwear, he watched Gabe take off his shirt and pull up his jeans. "You've got the sexiest chest and stomach. I could lick it from morning 'til night and still not get enough."

Gabe smiled and flexed his huge muscles in a mock bodybuilder pose. "Like that, do ya? Ask me later and I'll flex my butt muscles for ya." He disappeared down the hall and came back with a dark gray t-shirt that said Navy on the front.

Rex licked his lips. "So tell me what Jake said."

Gabe laughed and shook his head. "Well, he said he was interested but he'd have to talk to his foreman and then he told Cree to stop sucking his cock while he was trying to conduct business. I have a feeling Cree didn't listen to him because the end of our conversation was pretty much just a bunch of moans and groans. He should be calling back in a couple hours though. In the meantime maybe we should start herding some of the cattle closer to the ranch and start weeding out those we want to keep."

Rex filled a thermos with coffee and handed it to Gabe, then filled one for himself. "Let's go, sweetheart. The faster we get our work done, the faster we can play."

* * * * *

By lunchtime Rex and Gabe had selected about fifty head and drove them to the pasture closest to the barn. Gabe rode his horse toward Rex. "I'm going inside to see if Jake's called back and start lunch." He leaned sideways in the saddle and pulled Rex forward by the back of the neck and kissed him deeply. "Could you do me a favor and take Lolly's saddle off and give her a quick rubdown?"

Rex raised one eyebrow and kissed him again. "Sure thing, boss. I aim to please."

Gabe shook his head as they rode toward the barn. "Yeah, you please me all right."

Gabe jumped out of the saddle and handed the reins to Rex. "Lunch in thirty minutes, baby." Gabe jogged to Rex's house and took the stairs two at a time. When he got in the kitchen he checked the answering machine. He had two messages. The first one was from Jake telling him he'd be sending a couple of semis out tomorrow to pick up a hundred head. He said Ben was interested in fifty but he wanted twenty-five steers and twenty-five heifers. That only left Gabe fifty that he had to find a buyer for.

The second message was from the feed store telling Cotton his order was ready to pick up. Gabe erased the messages and started building sandwiches for himself and Rex. It would be a long afternoon if Rex had to run to the feed store and they still had to round up another hundred head of cattle. He decided maybe they'd just round up the cattle right after lunch and then head to town to pick up supplies. That way they could have dinner in Styler.

Gabe put the sandwiches on the table along with some of Rex's homemade potato salad and chips. He was making a new pitcher of brewed tea when Rex walked through the door.

He came up behind Gabe and wrapped his arms around him. "Did you hear from Jake?"

Gabe finished stirring the tea and turned around in his arms. "Yeah. He said he'd have his men come and get one hundred for him and another fifty for Ben. That just leaves us with fifty to get rid of and the feed store called and said your order was ready." He leaned in and kissed Rex, working his fingers into the thick black hair at the base of his neck. "I thought we could select the other hundred head right after lunch and then go in to Styler for the supplies together. I know they stay open until seven so it should give us plenty of time to get there. After we pick up the supplies I thought we could stop somewhere and get a bite to eat."

Rex kissed Gabe again and cupped his cock. "That all sounds good but we need to make sure we get home early enough to play. Also, would there be any way we could see my mom before we eat? Visiting hours are over at eight-thirty so we'd need to go there before we eat."

Gabe groaned and pushed him back toward the table. "Well, then we'd better get a move on. I can go to the grocery store while you visit your mom." Gabe picked up a sandwich and put it on his plate along with potato salad and chips. He took a bite of his sandwich and looked up. Rex was looking at him funny. "What? Did I say something wrong?"

Rex filled his plate and looked at him again. "Why don't you want to meet my mom?"

Gabe shrugged and took another bite of sandwich. "I just figured it would make you uncomfortable." He looked at Rex closely. "Unless you're just going to introduce me as your boss. I didn't mean to hurt your feelings, baby. I just don't know anything about having a mom."

Rex reached across the table and took Gabe's hand. He waited until Gabe stopped eating and looked at him. "My mom has always known I'm gay, sweetheart. I just wanted to introduce the two of you. I've got a feeling you're going to be around a while."

"Oh. Okay, I'd like to meet her."

* * * * *

Rounding up the rest of the cattle Jake's men were picking up tomorrow took the rest of the afternoon. By the time they hauled a load of water to the tanks for them and got cleaned up it was six o'clock. They jumped into the flatbed farm truck and drove the eighteen miles to Styler. They backed up to the dock of the feed store at six-thirty.

While Rex took care of business there, Gabe ran to the grocery store for a few things. He bought a couple of bags of ice to put into the cooler strapped to the back of the flatbed. He put the bacon, milk, cheese and lunchmeat in the cooler and the rest of the nonperishables up front in the cab.

Rex finished his business and they were on their way to the nursing home by seven o'clock. Rex parked the big truck at the back of the parking lot. He got out and started walking toward the building. He must have noticed Gabe wasn't following because he stopped and turned around. Gabe couldn't move from his seat.

Rex came back to the truck and opened the passenger door. "What's going on, Gabe?" Rex put his hand on Gabe's shoulder and squeezed.

Gabe shook his head. "I don't know. I just can't seem to move. I guess it's nerves. I mean, I've never met anyone's mother before. I…I'm afraid I'll say all the wrong things and she won't like me and then you won't like me. I don't know how to explain it to you, Rex. I just don't want to screw this up between us."

Rex leaned in the door and kissed him. He actually thrust his tongue down Gabe's throat right there in the parking lot. Rex stood back up straight. "Come on, get out of the truck, sweetheart. My mom's going to love you as much as I'm beginning to."

Gabe let Rex pull him out of the truck. They walked hand in hand inside the nursing home and to room 123. Rex knocked on the door and stuck his head in. "Mom, I've come to visit and I brought someone special to meet you."

Maggie Cotton smoothed the quilt on her lap and patted her hair. "Come in, dearest boy. I'd love to meet your friend."

Rex pulled a very nervous Gabe into the room. He bent over and gave his mom a warm embrace and a kiss on the cheek. He held out his hand for Gabe to come closer. "Mom, I'd like you to meet Gabe Whitlock. He's the new owner of the Double B and someone very special to me." Rex stood back up and put his arm around Gabe.

Maggie held out her small, frail hand. "Very nice to meet you, Mr. Whitlock."

Gabe held her tiny hand in his big one. He was so afraid of hurting her that instead of shaking her hand he bent over and kissed it. "It's a pleasure to meet you, Ms. Cotton, and please call me Gabe."

Maggie giggled like a schoolgirl at his kiss on her hand. "Only if you call me Mom or Maggie."

Gabe blushed and turned to look at Rex. "I'd be happy to call you Maggie but Mom would be a little uncomfortable for me right now." Gabe took Rex's hand and squeezed.

Rex squeezed back and sat down on a straight-back chair. "Can we do anything for you while we're here, Mom?" Rex motioned for Gabe to take the other chair beside him.

"Hmm...actually there is. Could you do me a favor and sneak me a candy bar? Every time I get close to the dern candy machine the nurse on duty pushes me back in here. I don't understand why I can't have a bar of chocolate. It's not like I'm diabetic or anything. I think it's just a little torture game they play with the residents."

Gabe couldn't help but smile. He looked at Rex and Rex nodded his head. Gabe stood up. "What kind of candy bar would you like, Maggie?"

Maggie smiled like a child on Christmas morning. "Just a plain chocolate bar please, with no nuts or anything else. Just plain chocolate."

Gabe laughed and winked at her. "I may have to make a couple trips around the building to throw the nurses off their game but I'll accomplish my mission. You've got my word." He winked at Rex and left the room.

Rex watched him go with a smile. He turned back to his mom who was giving him the mom look. "What?"

Maggie patted his hand. "You're falling in love with him, aren't you, dearest boy?"

"Yes, I am, Mom. He seems like such a strong man. He was a Navy SEAL for eight years but his heart is so vulnerable. The reason he can't call you Mom is because he hasn't had one since his own abandoned him in front of a drugstore when he was three. He grew up being bounced from foster home to foster home. Besides his ex-SEAL buddies I don't think anyone has ever really cared for him. I want to give him a home with me but I've only known him for a month really and we've only been intimate since yesterday. So why do I have such strong feelings for him already?"

"You, son, are just like me. I fell in love with Martin Cotton the minute I laid eyes on him and we married two months later. I know you may not have a very high opinion of your father but despite the alcohol he was a good man. I'll never love another until the day I die. You and I are alike in that respect also. If you fall in love with this man you'll love him until your last breath. Just go with your heart, not your head. Heads seem to talk a lot of people out of taking risks and a lot of people miss out because of it."

Rex leaned over and gave his mom another kiss. "I love you, Mom."

Just then the door opened and Gabe made a big production of sneaking in. He slid up next to Maggie and opened a newspaper. Inside were about seven candy bars. "I struck the mother lode, Maggie. Now I know your chocolate craving will be satisfied until we can get back into town."

Maggie winked at Gabe and took one of the candy bars and slipped it into the side pocket of her wheelchair. "Where can we hide the rest? I know if we don't those nosy nurses will steal them."

Gabe looked around the room. "Hmmm...got it." Gabe went over to the table and picked up the silk flower arrangement that sat on top of it. He pulled the flowers out and took the piece of foam out of the vase. He carefully put the candy bars inside the large vase and put the bouquet of flowers back into the vase. Gabe set the vase back on the table. "*Voila*, an instant storage facility for your contraband."

Maggie made a big production of clapping and cheering. "You're so clever, Gabe." She held her hand out to him again. Gabe took it, a little more comfortable with her now. "Thank you. Chocolate is my only indulgence these days. Now if only I could talk you into a Big Mac and fries." She chuckled and winked at Gabe.

Rex stood up and kissed his mom's cheek. "I'd better get Gabe out of here before he starts promising you the moon. Have a good week, Mom, and we'll try to come back Thursday evening."

Maggie kissed him back and patted his hands. "I love you, dearest boy."

"I love you too, Mom. Just remember...only one chocolate bar a day. I don't want you to get thrown out of this joint."

Gabe looked at Maggie for a minute and bent and kissed her cheek. "I'll see you Thursday, Maggie."

"Goodbye, dearest Gabe."

They left the nursing home and drove to Chester's Bar and Grill. Rex pulled the truck up to the side of the building and he and Gabe went inside. They sat at a back booth and ordered dinner and a beer. While they were waiting for their food Rex got up and put some money in the jukebox. He selected his songs and sat back down.

A slow George Strait song was the first to come up. Rex looked at Gabe and nudged him with his foot. "I wish this was the kind of town where I could pull you up and dance with you."

Gabe nudged him back. "I'll dance with you when we get home, baby."

Rex signaled the waitress for two more beers and finished his off. "I forgot to tell you. I heard something interesting in the feed store today. I asked Jack Webber if he knew of anyone who'd be interested in buying fifty head of cattle and he not only gave me a couple names but he told me something else that sounds very interesting. When I told Jack about our water dilemma he casually said it was too bad those oil wells Buck had drilled didn't come through. I asked him what he was talking about and it seems about twenty-eight years ago Buck brought some geologist out to the Double B to find oil. I guess the geologist was sure there was oil on the eastern side of the ranch but when they drilled they found only small traces of oil. Finally Buck ran out of money at about thirty thousand feet so he had to stop drilling. He had the hole plugged up and wrote off his losses as a bad investment, but according to Jack the geologist was positive there was oil down there."

The waitress brought their dinners and another round of beer. Gabe rubbed his scratchy jaw. "How much farther down do you think someone would need to go to find it?"

Rex shook his head. "I've no idea but I was thinking maybe it'd be worth it to bring in another geologist to study the thing. I know the well had to be capped when they didn't find anything but it may not be that hard to open up. We'd need a geologist to tell us that stuff."

Eating his hamburger, Gabe thought about what Rex told him. "Where do we find a geologist that we can afford?"

Rex ran his fingers through his hair. Gabe noticed he did that a lot when he was thinking hard. "We can get a graduate student to come down for the rest of the summer. It would be good experience for them and a hell of a lot cheaper for us."

Gabe smiled. "Us, does that mean you're going to go in on it with me?" Gabe took another bite of his hamburger.

"Of course I'd go in on it. I've got a little money saved and I can't think of a better cause than the save my home charity."

"What college would you call?"

Rex shrugged his shoulders. "I don't know I guess I could just call the college in Tulsa and ask for the geology department and take it from there. Maybe you could go online tomorrow and see if you can find out a professor's name in the geology department and we could call him directly."

"Sounds like a plan. I can't believe I'm seriously thinking of drilling for oil." Gabe paid the tab and they left the bar.

Chapter Four

ꕥ

After another long passion-filled night Gabe was sound asleep when Rex shook him. "Get up, sweetheart, I hear semis coming down the road. Those boys must have left in the middle of the night to get here this early."

Groaning, Gabe turned over and yawned. "I was hoping for a little action this morning but the way my balls feel it's probably a good thing the truck is here early."

Rex pulled Gabe in for a deep morning kiss. "Did this old fella wear you out last night? I'll just have to be a little more careful from now on."

Gabe smiled and smacked his ass. "I don't know that it was so much you as it was the kitchen counter and the bed of the truck and the shower. My poor cock isn't used to fucking on every available surface—yet. Give me a few more days of practice and I'll be able to keep up with the best of 'em."

Laughing, Rex got out of bed and pulled a pair of jeans on. He realized what he was doing and looked over at Gabe. "Damn, now you've got me going without underwear." He chuckled and pulled a snap-front shirt out of the closet. He'd cut the sleeves off his shirt years ago and it was pretty threadbare but Rex loved it anyway. He pulled socks on and headed out the door. "Get up, you're wastin' daylight, sweetheart."

Gabe grumbled a little more and got up and got dressed. He watched Rex, shaking his head as he left the room.

By the time he got outside, Jake's men were already starting to load the cattle. He spotted Rex talking to Jake's foreman, Hank. He walked over and joined them. He reached out and shook Hank's hand. "Hi, Hank. Thanks for getting here so soon. It'll save me from hauling water to them today."

Hank tipped his hat in typical cowboy fashion. "Hi, Gabe. Jenny sent you a batch of chocolate chip cookies. They're in the truck."

Gabe's eyes lit up. He immediately walked over to the semi and retrieved the cookies. He took them back to Rex. "You've got to try these. Jenny makes the best cookies in the world. She never would share her recipe with me but as long as she keeps sending 'em my way I won't complain too loudly."

Reaching into the bag, Rex pulled out a handful of cookies. When he saw Gabe's eyebrows shoot up he shrugged. "I told you I had a major thing for sweets." He winked and Gabe blushed and turned away from Hank.

After the cattle were loaded and the bill of sale signed Rex gave Hank a total dollar amount and Hank wrote him out a Triple Spur check. Hank waved out the window and drove off in a cloud of dust. Rex handed the check to Gabe. "Don't spend that all in one place. We're going to have to tighten our belts a little more if we're really planning on drilling for oil. At least we only have half as many animals to feed this winter."

Gabe took the check and sighed. It was a lot of money but Gabe knew the drilling would be expensive and with only half a herd if they didn't find oil things could get rough. Gabe folded the check and put it in his back pocket. He looked over at Rex. "What's up for the rest of the day?"

Rex took off his hat and ran his long, tapered fingers through his thick hair. He settled the hat back on to his head and smiled at Gabe. "Well, truthfully I'd like to fuck that sweet ass of yours for the rest of the day but there's plenty of work to do and I have a feeling that sweet ass needs a little break. I guess I'll take a couple of the big round bales to the remaining herd and check the water levels in the tanks. I've got a fence that needs a little work in the south pasture so that should take care of the rest of my afternoon. What about you? Are you gonna call the university?"

"That's an awfully long speech just to tell me to keep my hands off you." Gabe smiled and walked into Rex's arms. "I think you're right though. My ass isn't hurting so much as my poor balls. So I guess I'll go search the internet and find what I can at the University of Tulsa. I also want to dig into some of Buck's old files. Maybe I can find something on the oil well. Matter of fact, I think it would be best if I did that first." He ran his tongue up the side of Rex's sweaty face. "Tonight my balls should be just fine, so save some of that strength of yours today, baby." Gabe reached around and squeezed the twin globes of Rex's ass.

Gently thrusting his cock at Gabe, Rex sighed. "How am I supposed to get on Chief if my dick's hard? Do you have any idea how painful that can be?"

Gabe laughed and kissed him again. "I've some idea how that feels. I rode around this ranch with a hard-on for the past month." Gabe kissed him and headed for Buck's office in the main house. He turned back once and waved to Rex and set off to find the key to their future.

Gabe walked into the house and once again he felt like he needed a shower. The place just felt damn dirty. He knew Jake and Jenny had both pretty much grown up here but it was Buck and his sick mind that made the house dirty. He walked down the hall and entered Buck's office. He hadn't really touched anything in here since he'd moved in. Gabe preferred to do his books at the kitchen table on his laptop.

Gabe walked over to the file cabinet and tried to open the drawer. Of course, leave it to Buck Baker to lock the damn cabinet and then get shot. Gabe had no idea where the fucking key was. He found a screwdriver under the sink in the kitchen and pried the lock off.

He knew that the files he was looking for were old so he started in the bottom drawer. He skimmed the files until his eyes stopped on one file labeled "Jenny". Curiosity got the better of him and he pulled out the file. What he found inside made bile rise in his throat. He threw the file down on the desk and ran to the bathroom.

Washing his mouth out in the bathroom sink, Gabe leaned heavily against the sink. He knew he'd have to call Cree but goddamn it, Buck was dead. Maybe he'd ask Rex what he thought. He left the bathroom and went back into the office, keeping his gaze averted from the file on the desk.

He found nothing in the files but they all seemed to be from the past ten years. Gabe wondered where the rest of the files were stored. A sickening thought finally struck him—the basement. Buck probably stored the old files in the basement. The same basement where Buck held Jenny captive after his most recent kidnapping.

Gabe wiped his sweaty hands on his jeans as he stood at the top of the stairs. He swallowed a few times and walked down the steps. The room Jenny had been kept in was to the right. The door Cree and Jake broke in to get to Jenny still sat on the floor. The wood was splintered around the doorframe.

Passing by the room with only a brief glance, Gabe made his way to the back of the old basement. He found a room full of boxes and old furniture. He turned on the light and was rewarded when two bare bulbs hanging from the ceiling shed a minimal amount of light into the creepy room.

Going through his fifth box Gabe was about to give up the search for the day when something caught his eye, a file labeled "Buck's Folly". Gabe pulled the file out and opened it. The contents made him whoop with joy. He'd finally found what he was looking for and he could get out of this house.

He grabbed up the file and turned off the lights. Gabe practically ran up the stairs and out the front door. Walking through the kitchen door at Rex's house, he sank into the nearest chair and exhaled the breath he'd been holding. He opened the file and spread it out on the table. He studied the file for about an hour and then retrieved his laptop.

The University of Tulsa had a Geoscience department and the site listed the head of the department along with his direct office number. Gabe took the phone off the wall and punched in the phone number.

"Dr. Milton Raymore's office, how may I help you?"

"Um…hi, my name is Gabe Whitlock and I was wondering if I could speak with Dr. Raymore about hiring one of his grad students for the rest of the summer?" Gabe crossed his fingers that the secretary would put him through.

"I'm sorry, sir, but Professor Raymore is doing research in Louisiana for a paper and won't be back at the university for another two months."

Gabe couldn't help but sigh. "Oh, okay. Well…I'm sorry to have bothered you, ma'am."

"Wait. Maybe I can help you, Mr. Whitlock, and please call me Alice. I happen to know all of the professor's grad students and I might have a candidate for you. What exactly would you like this student to work on?"

"Thanks for your help, Alice, but to be totally honest I don't really know. I recently bought a ranch in western Oklahoma and I just found out that there may be oil on the ranch. It seems the previous owner had a geologist down here almost thirty years ago and they drilled but didn't come up with enough evidence as to the size of oil deposit so the owner capped the well and wrote it off. I was hoping to get a geologist down here to see what he thinks about the possibility of oil. And to be perfectly honest I can't afford a full-fledged geologist so a friend suggested a grad student."

Gabe could hear the smile in Alice's voice as she hummed to herself. "I think I might have the perfect student for you, Mr. Whitlock. Boone Fowler. He's one of the brightest young men I've seen come through this department. He's a bit of a loner but I'm sure he'd welcome some on-site experience. If you can give me your phone number I'll call Boone and have him return your call if he's interested in the job."

Gabe almost jumped up and down like a kid. "Oh Alice, you don't know how happy that would make me." Gabe gave her his phone number and thanked her again.

He was feeling much better now than when he came out of the main house. It was like night and day. Gabe decided to get some steaks out of the freezer to thaw for supper. He thought he'd make fajitas. He looked into the cupboards and the fridge to make sure he had all the ingredients he'd need and turned on the radio.

* * * * *

Gabe was doing some major hip shaking when a dirty, tired Rex strolled through the door twenty minutes later. Rex grinned and walked up behind Gabe, ready to capture him in his arms when suddenly Gabe spun around and his hand grabbed Rex's throat. Rex would never forget the look in his eyes.

Immediately Gabe let go of Rex's throat and closed his eyes. "I'm sorry, baby. I…uh…you can't sneak up on me from behind like that. I could have killed you." Gabe looked down and shrugged. "Sometimes the training takes over. I'm sorry."

Rex pulled him into his chest and kissed the top of his head. "It was my fault, sweetheart. There's nothing to be sorry for. I just saw that fantastic ass of yours shaking and didn't think before I walked up behind you. I'll make sure I at least clear my throat before I try to molest you from now on."

Those words threw Gabe mind back to Buck's office. He reached for Rex, suddenly feeling nauseous again. Gabe's stomach roiled and he excused himself and ran to the bathroom.

Rex was leaning against the table when he reemerged from the bathroom. "Want to talk about it?"

Gabe went straight to his arms. He pressed his face into Rex's hair and held on tight. "I found a file in Buck's office today. A file that no one but Buck knew existed. A file on Jenny."

Rex put his hands on either side of Gabe's head and forced him into eye contact. "What kind of file?"

Gabe started feeling dizzy just thinking about what he'd found. He'd seen a lot of gruesome sights in his ten years in the Navy but nothing to prepare him for the pictures in that file. He pulled away and walked around the breakfast bar to the living room. He sat on the couch and held his hand out to Rex. Rex joined him and pulled Gabe once again into his embrace. "Talk to me, sweetheart."

Nodding, Gabe got even closer to Rex and swallowed. "We all knew Buck was a sick fuck but the file I found would make anyone else, well…throw up. It was pictures of Jenny and journal entries about her. It seems Buck had some sort of peephole into Jenny's bedroom. There were pictures taken as early as the age of twelve or thirteen. Mostly naked pictures taken when Jenny was obviously getting ready to shower or get ready for bed or something. They span the years until she was I assume eighteen." Gabe blew out a breath and ran his fingers through his hair. "But that's not all. He had pictures of him raping her. He took naked pictures after he'd beaten and branded her. It looked like she was unconscious but he took the time to pose her in provocative positions. I didn't dare read the journals. I was afraid for my own soul after seeing the pictures. There was no way I could read the writings of someone so incredibly evil and still retain my sanity." Gabe looked into Rex's eyes and kissed him. "What do you think I should do with the file? Should I just burn it or should I call Cree and ask him what's best?"

Rex clenched his jaw so hard he thought his teeth might break. "Burn them. Buck's dead and unless you want Cree to dig him up and kill him again I'd say burn them. Jenny's trying to get on with her life. She has Cree and Jake and the twins she's carrying. Let's just let them live in peace and take care of this one last thing for them." Rex ran his hand down Gabe's back.

Gabe needed to be closer. He stood up and repositioned himself so that he was straddling Rex's lap. He sat down and pulled Rex's head closer and devoured his mouth. After several minutes of tonsil hockey he leaned back. "Could you go with me to get the pictures?"

Rex ran his fingers through Gabe's short brown hair. "I'll do better than that, sweetheart. I'll get them by myself. I don't want you anywhere near that house right now."

Nodding his head, Gabe leaned in for another kiss and began unsnapping Rex's work shirt. He smoothed his hands over the still-firm muscles of Rex's chest, twirling his fingers through the now-gray chest hair. He ran his fingertip around the dark brown areola and watched in fascination as bumps began to sprout out and the little dark brown nipple plumped up, begging for his tongue. Gabe lowered his mouth and swiped his tongue over the pouting nub.

Rex groaned and sat back even farther into the comfortably deep leather couch. Rex spread his thighs to make room for his growing cock, which it so happened spread Gabe's thighs wider too. "I love your mouth, sweetheart." He put his hand on the back of Gabe's head and held him to his chest.

Gabe's cock was so hard he thought it might pop the metal buttons on his jeans. He remembered that Rex had gone without underwear today and it was just too much temptation to resist. He latched his mouth on Rex's nipple and sucked hard. In the meantime his hands wandered down to Rex's splayed thighs and then back up to massage his cock through the denim.

When Rex groaned a little louder Gabe carefully unzipped Rex's jeans and pulled his cock free, mindful of the sharp teeth of the zipper. He pulled off Rex's nipple and looked down and then looked into his eyes. "Zippers can be very dangerous if you don't wear underwear, that's why all my jeans button." He winked and went back to suckling Rex's hard nub.

Lifting Gabe, Rex stood up beside the couch. He toed off his work boots and unbuttoned Gabe's jeans. Gabe's cock sprang right out of the tight-fitting jeans and into Rex's hand. "I want to taste you." Without another word between them Rex pulled his jeans off the rest of the way and Gabe did the same. Rex reached for Gabe and removed the gray Navy t-shirt and stretched him out on the couch.

Rex put his knees on the couch above Gabe's head and leaned over until Gabe's cock hit him in the chin. Rex rubbed Gabe's cock and Gabe rubbed Rex's. Soon they were lost in licking, sucking and moaning. They timed their thrusts perfectly so both men got exactly what they needed to come.

Gabe lost the battle first and exploded his essence down Rex's throat. The taste was so erotic to Rex he gave up the fight soon after and rewarded Gabe with a bellyful of cum. They licked each other clean and Gabe turned around and snuggled into Rex's side. They were almost asleep when the phone rang.

Rex raised his head. "Damn, I was comfortable." He started to get up but Gabe pushed him back down.

He got off the couch and headed for the phone. "It could be the grad student I left a message for." He picked up the receiver in the living room. "Hello."

"Yes, is Mr. Whitlock available?"

"Speaking."

"Hi, I'm Boone Fowler. Alice asked me to give you a call concerning a job?"

Gabe took the cordless phone over to the couch and sat at Rex's side. The deep voice on the other end of the phone already had his cock filling. "Thanks for calling, Mr. Fowler. I'm interested in having a geologist's opinion on an oil well that was dug almost thirty years ago. It was capped when the then owner believed there wouldn't be enough oil found to offset the cost of casing and cementing it. I was wondering whether you'd be interested in a summer job evaluating the well. We can't pay a lot but I was thinking five hundred a week plus room and board."

"I'm very interested in the job, Mr. Whitlock. Would you like me to email you some references?"

Gabe tensed at that deep voice again. What was it about that voice that made Gabe's cock tingle? Rex rubbed Gabe's muscled biceps and leaned in to kiss them, momentarily distracting Gabe from Boone's question. "Um…no, actually. You've already come highly recommended by Alice so that's good enough for me. When can we expect you?"

"Anytime you'd like. I can be there as early as tomorrow morning if you'll give me some directions to your ranch."

Rex leaned up and captured Gabe's nipple with his mouth, gently biting the pale brown nub. "That would be great. Can I call you Boone? Please call me Gabe." Gabe went on to give Boone directions to the ranch.

"I should be there by around ten in the morning. In the meantime see if you can find a topographical map of the area."

"Will do. Bye, Boone." Gabe hung up the phone and leaned down to kiss Rex. "Remember when we agreed to go easy on my balls today? Well, you, mister, are not holding up to the agreement." He laughed and pounced on top of Rex. "I was going to make fajitas for dinner but at this rate we'll have to settle for a late-night steak."

Chapter Five

ഗ

The next morning Gabe was mucking out the stalls and feeding the horses when an old light blue pickup pulled into the yard. Gabe looked at his watch. Nine-forty, the kid must be anxious. He put down the pitchfork he'd been using and walked out into the early morning sunshine. He waved his hand toward the truck. The shadowy figure in the truck waved back.

Gabe watched as Boone got out of the old beat-up truck and strode toward him. "Fuck me," Gabe whispered to himself. Boone Fowler wasn't the young nerdy geologist he'd pictured. Instead six feet of hard, muscled sex on a stick strode toward him. Boone must have been at least in his late twenties if not early thirties. Gabe noticed the way his long blond ponytail whipped around in the dry hot wind. As he got closer the blue of his eyes almost knocked the breath out of Gabe.

He finally managed to not only shut his mouth but to also get his legs to move and went to meet his new employee. When Gabe was only a couple of feet from him he stuck out his hand. "You must be Boone. I'm Gabe Whitlock. Welcome to the Double B."

Boone grasped Gabe's hand in a firm handshake. "Thanks. It looks like a great place." Boone pointed toward the main house. "Fantastic old farmhouse you've got there."

Gabe dropped Boone's hand. "Yeah. Well, that's something Rex and I wanted to talk to you about. Why don't I show you to his house and get you a cold drink and then I'll go find Rex. I believe he's still in the basement of the main house looking for maps."

Boone nodded and followed Gabe into Rex's house. Gabe kept getting the strange feeling that Boone was staring at his ass but there was no way this hot hunk of human flesh could be gay. Gabe motioned to a chair and opened the fridge. "I've got beer, tea or lemonade."

Boone took off his baseball hat and sat it on the table. "Um…lemonade would be great, thanks."

Gabe poured Boone a glass of lemonade and sat it on the table in front of him. "I'll get the file I have on the well. I'm not trying to hurry you along but I'm not sure how long it will take to track down Rex." Gabe watched as Boone took a long drink of his lemonade. He was mesmerized by the tendons in Boone's neck. Boone caught him looking and smiled. "Well…uh…I'll just go get Rex. Feel free to get more lemonade."

Gabe left the kitchen in a hurry. What the hell was wrong with him? Yeah, Boone was like the hottest thing since…Rex. Fuck, he was so screwed. And that voice. Good Lord in heaven, that voice spoke to his erection something fierce. How could he possibly be attracted to two men at the same time? Besides the fact that he loved Rex. He knew it in his heart that he loved that man. For the first time in his entire life he had a home and someone to love so why was just the sound of Boone Fowler's voice enough to make his dick hard?

Gabe walked up the steps to the main house. He knew he'd have to talk to Rex about his screwed-up thoughts, eventually. Right now they had to decide what to do about the living arrangements regarding Boone. They hadn't really discussed it yet.

He walked in the front door and headed toward the basement steps. He peered down into the basement. "Rex? Are you down there?"

"Yeah. I'll be up in a minute, sweetheart. Just stay up there. I'll meet you out on the porch."

Gabe left the house and sat down on the porch swing. He looked out over the pasture and began to wonder about the oil. What would he do if they really did find oil out there? The answer came to him with a smile. Burn this fuckin' house down to the ground and rebuild it. That's exactly what he'd do if he ever had the money. He could even invite Jenny, Jake and Cree to roast marshmallows over the coals of the burning house.

When Rex came out the front door Gabe had a silly-assed grin on his face. Rex looked at him and sat down. "What's so funny?" He leaned back in the swing and put his arm around Gabe.

"I was just thinking what I'd do if we really found oil out there. I came up with the perfect present for myself. I'd burn this den of evil to the ground and rebuild." Gabe looked over at Rex and smiled. "What would you do?"

Rex stretched his legs out and ran his hand up under his hat to his hair. "I'd find a way to bring my mom here. Build her a little house or something that's wheelchair accessible."

Gabe squeezed Rex's hand. "Maybe we can do that anyway, Rex. Let's see how this oil thing goes and then we can figure out our financial situation."

Rex looked at him jaw wide open. He shook his head and snapped it shut. "Seriously, Gabe? You wouldn't mind if Mom lived out here with us?"

Leaning in to give a nice warm kiss, Gabe smiled. "I plan on being with you for the rest of my life, Rex. I can't explain how it happened so damn fast but I love you. A big part of you is the love that you have for your mom. How could I object to her living out here? Besides I've never had a mom and I get the feeling your mom has enough mothering in her for both of us."

"I talked to my mom about you, Gabe. I told her I was falling in love but it didn't make sense to me because we've only known each other for a month and only been intimate for two days. She told me that's how fast she fell in love with my dad. She also told me that if I'm like her I'll love you until I draw my last breath." Rex looked over at Gabe and chuckled. "A couple of lovesick teenagers is what we're acting like but ya know, I don't care."

Gabe leaned in and kissed him. "We can be lovesick fools together."

Rex squeezed his shoulder where his hand rested on the swing behind Gabe's head. He jerked his head toward the blue pickup. "Boone here already?"

Gabe swallowed, "Yeah. He got in about fifteen minutes ago. I sat him at the kitchen table with the file and a glass of lemonade and came to find you. We need to discuss where he's going to stay."

Rex looked confused. "Well, that's a no-brainer. He'll have to stay in the house with us. I've got a spare room now that I'm keeping you in mine." Rex looked toward the main house. "I wouldn't ask anyone to sleep in there. Unless you think the kid will be uncomfortable with the two of us sharing a room?"

Wiggling in his seat, Gabe looked a little sheepishly at Rex. "Come to find out he's not at all what I'd imagined him to be. I thought a geologist grad student would be young and kind of nerdy but Boone is nothing of the sort."

Rex raised an eyebrow. "Go on."

Gabe licked his suddenly dry lips. "Well, first of all he's probably in his late twenties or early thirties." At Rex's continued attention Gabe swallowed and went on. "Oh hell, Rex. I don't know how else to say it but the man is sex on a stick but I want you to know you have absolutely nothing to be jealous of. I've been around good-looking men all my life and you're the first stud to capture my heart. I'm not stupid enough to ever jeopardize that. Do you get what I'm telling you? You're the man for me and just because you might catch me occasionally looking at someone else doesn't mean I want someone else, okay? Besides I've got a feeling you're going to be looking just as hard as I am. It's his eyes. They're like midnight blue. So blue they almost look black until the sunshine hits them. And his voice is so deep that it vibrates my cock every time he speaks. Anyway, tell me how we're going to tell him we're a couple and if it doesn't bother him he can take the extra room?"

Rex continued to look into Gabe's eyes. Finally he bent down and kissed him passionately. "I'd like you to know the same thing about me. I'll never cheat on you, no matter if I'm tempted or not. I love you, Gabe Whitlock, and I always will. Love at first sight seems to run in my family and my sight was set on you the first night I met you. Now, about Boone. I say we don't hide anything from him and just ask him if he'd rather stay with us or in the house of evil."

They got up off the swing. "Oh, I forgot. Did you find the map?"

Rex put his arm around Gabe as they walked down the steps. "Yes and no. I found a whole box of maps but I'm not really sure what Boone's looking for so I figured I could just show him the box and let him go through it." He kissed the side of Gabe's head. "By the way, what color hair does Boone have?" He smiled at Gabe and winked.

"Blond. Long honey blond hair."

"Oh fuck me." Rex groaned and squeezed Gabe a little tighter to his side.

"Those were my words exactly the first time I saw him. I'm afraid it's going to be a long, hot summer." He smiled back at Rex and pinched his ass.

Rex kissed Gabe one more time before they entered the house. He stepped through the front door with Gabe and saw immediately just how long a summer it was going to be. Gabe was right. The man in front of him was so hot. Boone was sitting at the kitchen table with the contents of the file spread out before him on the table. Boone looked up as he and Gabe entered the house. He had the cutest pair of reading glasses perched on the end of his nose.

Boone stood and walked over to the pair. Gabe stepped forward and gestured to Rex. "This is my partner, Rex Cotton. Rex, this is Boone Fowler."

Rex held out his hand and was surprised with the grip of Boone's handshake. He had the hands of a working man not an academic. "Nice to meet you, Boone. Why don't we all grab a cold drink and sit at the kitchen table, or we could go to the porch if you'd prefer."

Boone looked from Rex to Gabe. "Uh…the kitchen's fine with me. I'll need to clean the table a bit first though." He immediately started piling up papers and putting them back into the folder. "Did you happen to find the map I asked about?"

Grabbing a pitcher of iced tea out of the fridge, Rex nodded. He got out two glasses and filled them with ice as Boone continued to clean up the table and shut down his laptop computer. Rex caught himself looking at Boone's ass encased in a tight pair of faded jeans. He had a tiny hole at the corner of one pocket. Rex itched to stick his finger in that little hole. "I found a whole box of maps in the basement of the main house but I'm not sure which ones you're looking for so I thought you and I could take a look after we have a break." Rex filled the glasses and sat down beside Gabe. Boone sat across the table.

Rex could feel his hands starting to sweat. He kept looking at the long silky blond ponytail across from him and wondered what it would look and feel like down around Boone's shoulders. He shook his head slightly. What the hell was wrong with him? It was like he'd been put under some sort of spell. It was almost like Boone was supposed to be here, like the final piece of the puzzle.

He could hear Gabe asking Boone questions about the file he'd been looking through but Rex wasn't able to concentrate on the words. Gabe had been right about Boone's voice. It was so deep you had to concentrate to understand him. This was exactly the way he felt the first night he'd seen Gabe. What the fuck was he doing? He loved Gabe, he lusted for Gabe, so why couldn't he take his eyes off Boone?

Gabe turned to him and winked. "Isn't that right, Rex?"

Rex must have looked like a deer caught in the headlights, because Gabe seemed to know what was wrong with him. "Boone asked if we had any extra horses he could ride. I told him we had two workhorses, Bonnie and Clyde. Isn't that right, Rex?" Gabe winked and nudged his ribs with his elbow.

"Yeah, that's right. Bonnie is the sassy black mare and Clyde is the Appaloosa gelding. You're welcome to ride them anytime. Would you like to take a look at the barn now? That way we could show you where everything is stored so you can saddle up anytime you get a chance."

Boone grabbed his baseball hat off the table. "I'd appreciate that. One of the main reasons I decided to take the job was to be around horses again."

Rex and Gabe led the way to the barn. The horses had all been released to the corral earlier that morning so Gabe could muck the stalls. As they walked into the barn Gabe became a little red-faced at the mess in the aisle. "Sorry about the mess, Boone. I was mucking stalls when you pulled up and just kind of dropped everything, as you can clearly see." Gabe gestured to the wheelbarrow full of horse manure and old straw.

Gabe picked up the pitchfork and began finishing his morning chores. "Rex, why don't you show Boone where the saddles and tack are stored? Then take him out and introduce him to Bonnie and Clyde." At Rex's nod Gabe began cleaning out the next stall.

Rex ushered Boone toward the other side of the barn toward the tack room. He opened the door and stepped back. "Here's all the tack. Feel free to use anything you see on these two walls. My and Gabe's stuff is on the wall to the right so other than that you're good to go."

Boone looked at all the saddles lined up on saddle stands against two walls. "Why do you have so many saddles?"

"This ranch used to be owned by Buck Baker, hence the name the Double B. When Buck owned the farm we had about seven full-time cowboys working here. They were all day help. Most of them either had small ranches of their own or they lived in town. I've been the only full-time employee for years. I started working this ranch when I was barely legal. I was foreman for almost twenty-five years. These saddles all came with the ranch but it's just Gabe and me now."

Rex watched Boone walk over to the wall of saddles. He stopped in front of one and looked and touched the smooth leather and then moved on to the next one. He seemed to be lost in his own thoughts so Rex just stood there and ogled him.

After Boone had touched and looked at about seven saddles he finally selected one. It looked older than the rest of the saddles, black leather with white trim. "I'd like to use this one, if you don't mind?"

Rex must have given Boone a confused look because Boone explained himself without being prompted. "It reminds me of the saddle I had growing up. My grandpa gave it to me when I turned thirteen. He told me I was finally a man so I needed a man's saddle." Boone went back to his own thoughts again. Rex could see the vacant faraway look in his eyes.

Rex cleared his throat to get Boone's attention once more. "Did you grow up on a ranch?"

Boone nodded and stroked the saddle. "Yeah, down around Houston, Texas. My dad owned a big ranch down there."

Rex shifted his feet a little uncomfortable. "Well, if you'd like to have him send your own saddle up here I could help pay the freight."

Boone shook his head and put the saddle back on the stand. "I don't have it anymore. My younger brother Tim had an accident when he was three. He got behind a hay wagon and the driver didn't see him and backed over him. He severed his spinal cord and was a paraplegic after that." Boone continued to run his fingers along the saddle's stitching as he talked. "One day Tim asked me if I could help him ride a horse. He'd spent almost eight years of his life in a wheelchair. Tim said he wanted to know what it felt like to get around without the wheelchair. In his mind it would be as good as walking. So I told him I'd have to ask Dad and figure out how to keep him in the saddle."

Rex saw Boone's jaws clench and he turned away and looked out the small barn window. When he continued his story Rex could tell Boone was reliving the past, his voice a kind of dreamy monotone.

"When I asked my father if I could teach Tim how to ride he slapped me and told me to leave Tim in the wheelchair where he was safe. When I told Tim what Dad said he broke down and cried. He just wanted to feel like a normal boy for an afternoon. I couldn't stand to watch him cry so I promised him I'd find a way to get him on a horse.

"That night after supper I snuck out to the barn and got down my brand-new black saddle. I took the saddle to the tool room and began attaching leather straps off old leather harnesses to it. I worked on the saddle every evening in secret for four days and finally I thought I'd done it. I'd managed to rig a harness of sorts to hold my brother onto the saddle. The next day I asked the widow next door if I could please bring my horse and saddle over to her ranch and teach Tim how to ride. She didn't think it would be possible but said I could try."

Boone quit talking and Rex couldn't stand it. He needed to know what happened. "Were you able to teach him?"

"Yeah. Once we figured out how to get him on the horse he was able to stay on just fine with the saddle I'd rigged. We managed to sneak off our ranch almost every day. It wasn't hard. My dad never paid attention to us. Tim rode my horse for almost two years and then just before his thirteenth birthday he got pneumonia. His body wasn't able to fight it and they put him in the hospital. Tim knew he was going to die and he asked me to make a promise to him."

Boone wiped tears off his cheeks and took a handkerchief out of his pocket and blew his nose. Rex thought he heard another sniffle and looked behind him. Gabe was leaning against the doorframe, also with tears in his eyes. Rex reached a hand out to Gabe. Gabe took it and squeezed. Rex cleared his throat around the solid lump now fully formed. "What was the promise, Boone? Can you tell me?"

"He wanted me to stop hiding my true self from my father and to tell him I was gay. I was only seventeen but Tim and I both knew it. So I made my brother that promise and he died two hours later." Boone rested his arms down on the saddle and buried his face in his hands.

Rex looked at Gabe and they both moved toward Boone. They each put a reassuring hand on his shoulder and squeezed, letting him know they were there.

Boone wiped his eyes again and continued. "I made the mistake of telling my father the next day about the promise I'd made to Tim and about teaching him to ride my horse. My dad went straight to the barn and found my saddle. He put it in the center of the ranch yard and hacked it to pieces with an axe. He then calmly turned to me and told me to get off his ranch. That it was bad enough he'd had a cripple for a son, he would not stand for having a fag too." Boone blew his nose again and shrugged. "I snuck into the cemetery and hid behind a gravestone so I could be there for my brother's funeral. That was the last day I ever saw my father.

"I stayed with a friend in town until my eighteenth birthday and then joined the Army. I knew I wanted to go to college and the only way I'd be able to afford it was on the GI bill so I stayed in the army until I was twenty-three and then went to the University of Tulsa and well, you know the rest." He looked over his shoulder at Rex and then Gabe. "I'm sorry." Boone shook his head. "I don't know why I spilled my guts like that. I've never told another soul what I just told the two of you. I guess seeing the saddle brought it all back to me. I hope you don't think I'm some kind of wimp."

Rex softly patted Boone on the back. "Not at all. We all have skeletons in our closet. Sometimes the closet needs to be opened and aired out, that's all. Now if you're ready, why don't we go up to the main house and look for those maps?"

Boone nodded and walked toward the door. He stopped in the doorway and looked back. "Thanks."

Gabe and Rex nodded. Gabe kissed Rex softly on the cheek. "I'm going to finish up in here really quickly and go fix lunch."

Rex nodded and followed Boone to the main house. When they got to the porch Boone finally turned around. "Where's Gabe?"

Rex nodded toward the barn. "He's going to finish up his chores and go cook us some lunch. Besides, I don't like Gabe to come into this house. It upsets him."

Boone followed Rex up the porch stairs. "How could an old farmhouse upset him?"

Rex sighed and stepped into the foyer. "It's not so much the house itself but what has happened inside the house." Rex thought about the right way to explain the ordeal with Jenny. He finally decided on the truth. "Come on into the office and I'll explain it to you. I'm sure you'll hear all the grisly details in town anyway." Rex showed him into the office and told him the story of Jenny and Buck. Rex gestured to the pictures as he spoke. When he was finished Boone sat open-mouthed.

"How could you possibly work for a man like that for twenty-five years?"

Running his fingers through his hair, Rex looked into Boone's eyes. "I didn't know what Buck was really like. No one did. Not even Buck's own son knew what kind of evil lived in him. When Buck was killed, Jake and Jenny sold Gabe the ranch. Well, everything except my house which they signed over to me. Gabe tried staying in this house when he first got here but he got pretty close to Jenny when he guarded her and he says the house makes him feel dirty. I noticed a few days ago that he looked completely worn out and he told me he couldn't sleep in this house so that's when I invited him to stay at my place."

Rex looked at Boone, not really sure how far to go with the explanation. He finally realized that Boone had just bared his soul in the barn to two people he'd just met so it was only fair to do the same. "I fell in love with Gabe the first time I saw him but it took him moving into my house to put those feelings into actions. I came to find out Gabe seemed to feel the same way about me. I've never been happier in my life than I've been these past few days."

He paused and looked at Boone for any sign that he was disgusted or disappointed in Gabe and him. What he saw was a look of longing. "You can decide where you'd like to stay while you're here. I've got an extra room at my place or if you're a glutton for punishment you can stay here in the main house."

Boone rose from the sofa and walked around the office. "I agree with Gabe, this house has seen too much. I think I'd like to take you up on your offer to stay in your spare room, if you and Gabe don't mind. I don't want to get in your way."

Rex nodded and headed for the basement. "Don't worry about it, Boone. You're more than welcome to stay with us. Let's go to the basement and look at those maps so we can get the hell out of here."

Chapter Six

ꙮ

After a pleasant dinner and a couple of hands of poker Gabe and Rex left Boone in front of the maps he'd spread out on the kitchen table and went to bed. Rex was freshly showered and just getting into bed when Gabe stepped out of the shower. He dried his hair and threw the towel in the dirty clothesbasket. Gabe walked over to the wall and switched off the light. He crawled into bed and right into Rex's waiting embrace.

The two of them held each other for a while without talking, both lost in their own thoughts. Finally Rex kissed Gabe and pulled him even closer. "You feel it, don't you?"

Gabe smiled and ran his hand down the length of Rex's body, landing on the smooth-skinned erection. "Yeah, I feel it."

Rex chuckled and thrust up into Gabe's hand. "That's not what I meant and you know it." He kissed him one more time and fisted Gabe's growing erection. "There's something there between us. All three of us. It's more than Boone just being hot. It's a deeper connection."

Gabe slowly stroked Rex's cock. "Yeah, I feel it. I just can't wrap my mind around it. How can three alpha males possibly have this kind of effect on each other? What does it mean to the two of us?"

Rex rolled over on top of Gabe and rubbed his cock against Gabe's cock. He nipped and licked his way inside Gabe's sweet mouth. Gabe was right there with him. Rex spread Gabe's thighs a little more so he could get closer. He thrust and rubbed their cocks together until Gabe began to moan and thrust upward.

"Fuck me, baby. I need to feel your cock inside me. I need to become one with you." Gabe licked the side of Rex's face and wrapped his thighs around Rex's body.

Rex quickly reached over to the drawer and retrieved the lube. Gabe shook his head and kissed him. "Just slick up your cock and shove it in hard. I don't need you to stretch me tonight. I want to feel every loving inch of that beefy cock of yours."

Rex groaned and slicked his cock. He positioned himself at Gabe's hole and looked down at him. "If you keep talking like that I'm not going to last long, sweetheart." He shoved his cock past the ring of muscles and buried himself to the hilt. He didn't stop but immediately pulled out and shoved in again, hard. Rex continued the rhythm until Gabe's eyes rolled to the back of his head and his neck arched off the pillow. Rex bent down and bit the bulging tendon of Gabe's neck.

"Uhhh…gonna come…oh God, baby…feels so good…" Gabe thrust his ass hard one more time against Rex's cock and shot cum up his torso.

Rex sucked a mark on Gabe's neck and blasted his seed deep within Gabe on a howling scream. He collapsed on top of Gabe and licked his neck where he'd bitten. "Nothing will ever change the way I feel about you, sweetheart. Before we go any further in this discussion you have to know and understand that." He rose up and rolled to Gabe's side.

Gabe ran his fingers through Rex's thick graying hair. "I know that, baby, and you have to know I feel the same way but what are we going to do about Boone?"

Rex ran his hands around to squeeze Gabe's ass. "I say we see if he's receptive to joining our newfound family."

Gabe stopped and looked into Rex's dark green eyes. "How do we do that without freaking him out?"

Rex smiled and fingered Gabe's already sensitive hole as he spoke. "I don't know, maybe a tag team effort of subtle seduction. You know, a little wink here and brush of body there. Something innocent to most people but I've a feeling if Boone's at all interested he'll pick up on the vibes we're sending out."

Gabe pushed his ass into Rex's probing finger and was rewarded when it slipped inside to find his pleasure gland. "Oh baby, that feels good but I can't come any more or my balls will be as sore tomorrow as they were today."

Rex chuckled and pulled his finger out. He got up and looked back down at Gabe. "I'll go get us a warm rag and we can just hold each other until we fall asleep."

Gabe yawned and nodded and Rex went into the bathroom. He looked into the linen closet and found no clean washcloths. "Damn. I forgot to get them outta the dryer." He opened the door to the hallway, slowly looking to make sure all the lights were out and Boone was in bed. So far, so good, the house was completely quiet. He opened the door and started toward the laundry room off the kitchen. He grabbed a couple of washcloths out of the dryer and headed back through the kitchen.

Rex stopped at the fridge and picked up the milk carton. Gabe would go nuts if he saw this but what the hell. Rex tipped the milk carton to his mouth and took a big swallow. As he was putting the cap back on he heard a noise and spun around. Boone was standing in the doorway, eyes trained on Rex's half-hard cock silhouetted in the light of the refrigerator. Rex smiled and put the milk away and shut the door. "Don't tell Gabe you saw me drinking directly from the carton. He hates that."

Boone tried to act like the sight of a naked man wasn't affecting him but Rex could tell by the tent in his sweats that it did. "Sorry, man, I just got up to get a drink myself." Boone strode to the cupboard and got down a glass and filled it with water from the tap. He drank the entire glass and filled it again.

Rex thought he looked like a man dying of thirst. He walked over to the cupboard and got another glass down. He intentionally brushed his chest against Boone's arm as he reached for the glass. "I guess if you can be civilized then I can too." Rex heard Boone's inhalation and smiled to himself. "Care to join me for a glass of lemonade?" Rex casually walked back to the fridge and retrieved the pitcher of lemonade, leaving the door open long enough for Boone to get a look at his impressive erection. He took the pitcher of lemonade to the table and sat down.

Boone dumped the rest of the water in his glass down the drain and brought his glass to the table. Rex filled his glass and winked at him. "So tell me what you've found out from the maps?"

Boone put his glass down and cleared his throat. "We—well, I—think the original geologist who was brought in knew what he was looking for."

Rex watched as Boone slyly dropped his hand under the table and tried to adjust the growing erection in his sweats. Rex's cock was throbbing at the thought he affected Boone in this manner. He had the answer to his main question. Now he and Gabe would just have to figure out how to initiate physical contact. Rex spread his legs to give himself a little more room. His cock sprang up and almost hit the underside of the table.

Rex leaned back a little farther in the chair. If Boone really wanted to see his cock he'd be able to now. "So you think there really could be oil where they drilled the well almost thirty years ago?"

Boone shifted in his chair, clearly looking at Rex's cock now. "I can't say for sure. I'd need to ride up there and take a look for myself first." Boone unconsciously licked his lips and then met Rex's eyes.

Rex rubbed his chest, paying particular attention to the area around his nipples. "I'd love to ride with you. I'm sure Gabe would too. After the morning chores tomorrow we can do it." Rex emphasized the last four words.

He finished his lemonade and stood slowly, watching Boone out of the corner of his eye. He almost laughed at the look on Boone's face when he saw his full erection. Rex took the glass over to the sink and rinsed it out. He left it on the side of the sink and turned around. "Gabe and I are really glad you're here, Boone." Rex shoved off the counter and remembered to grab the washcloths as he left the kitchen.

He entered the bedroom and took the washcloths to the bathroom and ran hot water over one of them and returned to the bedroom. Just as he expected Gabe was sound asleep. Rex crawled under the covers and began washing Gabe's cock and asshole, paying special attention to his cock. Damn, he needed Gabe again or Boone but that would come in time. He bent over and took Gabe's cock in his mouth. The more he licked and sucked on the flaccid cock the more it seemed to grow.

Gabe moaned and thrust his cock down Rex's throat. "Are you trying to make me sore tomorrow, baby? 'Cuz if you don't stop now I'm gonna be."

Rex pulled off Gabe's cock and crawled up his body. He devoured Gabe's mouth. "We got him, I think."

Gabe's eyes opened wide. "Why, what happened?"

Rex told Gabe everything that happened in the kitchen. "That's why my damn cock is so hard." He looked deep into Gabe's gray eyes. "It felt so right, Gabe, I can't describe it. I think we've found another soul mate. I promised him we'd ride up to the oil well with him after chores in the morning."

Gabe kissed him. "You're very subtle, baby." Gabe laughed at Rex's bold moves in the kitchen. "I'll pack a lunch and we can have a picnic. Maybe take a little nap, if you know what I mean." Gabe reached down and started stroking Rex's cock. "I refuse to come any more tonight but maybe I can relieve you of this before I go back to sleep." Rex groaned and thrust into Gabe's fist. Gabe stroked faster and faster until Rex groaned and shot cum on to his hand.

Rex reached over the side of the bed and grabbed the still slightly warm washcloth and cleaned first Gabe's hand and then his own cock. He threw the rag down again and pulled Gabe into his arms. He kissed the top of his head. "Sleep, sweetheart. We have a man to catch tomorrow."

* * * * *

Boone went back to his bedroom and pulled his sweats off and got into bed. His cock was the longest and hardest it had ever been. He threw off the covers and wrapped his fingers as far around it as they would go. As he stroked himself he thought about Rex and Gabe.

What a difference a day could make. Before coming face-to-face with Gabe and Rex he'd always been a loner. He hadn't had any kind of emotional connection with anyone except Tim. Boone remembered his first look at Gabe. Damn, that man was sexy. His hair was a little shaggy but it worked for him and he loved Gabe's icy gray eyes. He had to be honest with himself and admit that he'd noticed Gabe's massive build before he ever got out of his truck. Gabe was standing in front of the barn with his tight faded jeans and his even tighter Navy t-shirt and Boone had instantly gone hard. He had to sit in his truck for a few extra minutes and recite the element chart to himself before he could even get out of the truck. Then as he walked toward the hulking mass of muscle and noticed his eyes. He knew then he was a goner.

Boone didn't think he'd ever seen a sexier man in his life until he met Rex. Rex was a totally different kind of sexy but sexy as hell all the same. With his weathered good looks and those deep green eyes Boone was lost twice in one day.

He still couldn't believe he'd told them about Tim and his father. He'd never even been tempted to bare himself like that but it seemed so natural to do it with those two men. He was a little disappointed when Rex outlined for him the relationship already established between him and Gabe, but he thought he could handle it. He tried his best to squelch the ache in his pants until he'd seen a naked Rex in the kitchen.

The thought of Rex's naked body got his fist moving even faster on his cock. He pumped and rubbed the head for moisture, using it as lube to ease his way. Boone noticed the way Rex's cock grew to a full erection during the time they were together. Maybe, just maybe, Rex wanted him as much as he wanted Rex, but where did that leave Gabe? Boone wanted Gabe just as much but didn't want to get between the two men. They honestly seemed to love each other and no way was Boone going to jeopardize that love.

Boone continued to pump but moved to his side so he could also finger his own hole. He pushed first two and then three fingers in and pumped his ass as fast as he was pumping his cock. The fingers in his ass caused a small bite of pain because it had been years since he'd allowed anyone to fuck him, but Boone needed the pain right now. He erupted onto the cool white sheets, calling Rex's and Gabe's names as he did. He quickly grabbed up the sweats and cleaned himself. He fell asleep with a smile on his face and his hand still on his cock.

Chapter Seven

ꕥ

The threesome headed toward the old oil well in the late morning sunshine. The day was already hot and only going to get hotter, Gabe thought. He looked over at Rex astride Chief and smiled. Gabe looked over in the other direction and made eye contact with Boone. Boone was looking sexier than ever today with his snug jeans, a tight red t-shirt and of course the ever-present baseball hat. He'd left his hair out of the ponytail holder but it was pulled through the back of his hat. Gabe itched to pull the hat off his head so he could watch that golden hair dance in the sunshine.

They crossed the east pasture in silence, the tension between the three of them slowly mounting. Boone stopped his horse every so often and looked at the land and the soil. They finally reached the site of the well about an hour after they'd set off. Boone climbed down from Clyde and dug out the maps and papers he had stored in his saddlebags. He opened the map and walked around the site.

Gabe looked at Rex and shrugged his shoulders. He got down off Lolly and found some shade to ground tie her. Gabe took care to unsaddle Lolly and brush her down before giving her a bowl with a canteen of water and a small pile of oats. He went back for Clyde and did the same as Rex followed him with Chief.

When the horses were taken care of, Gabe wrapped his arms around Rex and leaned in for a kiss. "I didn't think we were ever going to get here." He stopped to rub his cock. "My dick's been hard since we left."

Rex chuckled and kissed him again. "Yeah. Mine too and unless I'm mistaken Boone is having the same problem. Why don't we let him work for another half-hour and then start our 'picnic'? In the meantime let's find a cool spot to spread out the blanket. You did pack the king-sized quilt, didn't you?"

Gabe kissed Rex's worried brow. "Of course. I want a lot of room to play." Gabe walked off in search of another spot of shade. He'd never been this far into the ranch and felt like a kid exploring a new toy. He found the right spot and spread out the blanket. He dug out the sandwiches and grapes from his saddlebag. He'd have to find Rex for the drinks. He'd slipped those into Rex's bag.

Gabe found the two men standing closer than was really necessary, going over the map. Gabe smiled to himself and went to stand behind Rex. He wrapped his arms around him and leaned against him, his side brushing against Boone. "How's it going? Are you two ready to break for lunch?"

Rex reached back and squeezed Gabe's ass. "I'm definitely ready for our picnic, sweetheart. What about you, Boone?"

Boone noticed the hand on Gabe's ass and licked his lips. "Yeah, I could eat."

Gabe kissed the back of Rex's neck and led the two men to the picnic spot, stopping only to retrieve Rex's saddlebag. Rex immediately fell onto the quilt and spread out his long legs. He gestured for the saddlebag and began pulling out bottles of water for each of them.

When he leaned across the blanket to hand Boone his he made eye contact and held it. Boone reached for the bottle and placed his fingers over the top of Rex's. Rex stared into Boone's dark blue eyes and licked his lips.

Gabe almost choked. Could Rex be any more obvious? Gabe gave each man a sandwich and he sat behind Rex's head. He straddled his legs on either side of Rex's shoulders and Rex naturally lifted his head and put it on Gabe's throbbing cock. Gabe let slip with a small groaning sound and looked toward Boone.

Boone took a big drink of water and watched the two men in front of him. "Thanks for the lunch, Gabe. I guess I was hungrier than I thought." Boone took another bite of his sandwich and motioned toward the bag by Gabe's hip. "Are those grapes?"

Gabe smiled and picked up the bag. "Yes. Would you like one?" At Boone's nod Gabe withdrew one of the grapes and leaned over to put it in Boone's mouth, stopping to rub the fruit sensually over Boone's lips. Boone moaned and opened his mouth. Gabe put the grape as well as his fingers into Boone's warm mouth.

Boone closed his eyes and wrapped his mouth around Gabe's fingers. Gabe could feel Boone's tongue swirling around each of the two fingertips. Gabe groaned and leaned in farther, placing his mouth on Boone's, above his fingers.

Boone's eyes snapped open and allowed Gabe to withdraw his fingers. He licked at Gabe's lips and then stuck his tongue into Gabe's mouth. Gabe grabbed the back of Boone's head and pulled his lips even closer. Boone suddenly became aware of what he was doing and snapped his eyes toward Rex. He was surprised to see that not only did Rex seem to approve but he was stroking his cock through the denim of his jeans. His eyes were half-lidded and glued to the two of them.

At Rex's nod of approval Boone reached out and wrapped his arms around Gabe. He delved into Gabe's mouth for another passionate kiss and began to scoot closer. "Damn, you taste good, Gabe."

Gabe moaned and pushed him gently back onto the quilt and taking off his baseball hat. When he had Boone stretched out he ran his fingers through Boone's glorious hair and licked his neck. Gabe pulled the red t-shirt up over Boone's abdomen and groaned. "God, you're sexy. Take this off for me."

Boone quickly took off the t-shirt and then tugged on Gabe's. "You too. I wanna see all of you." He looked over at Rex. "C'mere and help us, Rex."

Rex got to his knees and removed Gabe's shirt and then his own snap-front shirt. He stretched his long body out on the other side of Boone. Rex leaned in and captured Boone's mouth in a deep kiss that went on forever. In the meantime, Gabe reached toward Boone's jeans and unbuttoned and unzipped them.

Rex began licking his way down Boone's neck while he reached over to undo Gabe's jeans but got hung up on the buttons.

Boone chuckled and slapped his hand away. "Please allow me." Boone used both hands to unbutton and then ease Gabe's jeans down, while kissing Gabe's chest.

In the next instant all three men broke apart and took off their own jeans and boots. Finally after they were all naked Boone looked from one man to the other. "Are you both sure about this? The last thing I want is to jeopardize what you two have going."

Rex's answer to the question was to bend over and swallow Boone's enormous cock. Boone's cock was the biggest by far that Rex had ever had in his mouth. Surprisingly Rex swallowed the big cock all the way down by totally relaxing his throat muscles and suppressing his gag reflex. He began to hum against the hard flesh in his mouth.

Boone moaned and thrust upward just a little, not wanting to choke Rex. "Oh…oh sweet Jesus, that feels good." He reached for Gabe and stuck his tongue down his throat, mimicking with his tongue what was being done to his cock.

Gabe moaned and reached for Rex's cock. He stared an easy pumping rhythm and continued to kiss Boone. Boone in turn started a stroking rhythm on Gabe's cock. The three became lost in a sensual haze of kissing and sucking until Boone broke the kiss with Gabe and groaned. "Gonna come…oh good… Ohhhh…yeah!" Boone exploded his thick white fluid down Rex's throat and watched Rex erupt in Gabe's hand.

Gabe lifted his hand to his mouth and licked Rex's seed. The taste of Rex was so good he shot his seed into Boone's waiting hand. Boone lifted his hand to suck off Gabe's essence as Rex licked his cock clean.

They fell back onto the blanket in a tangle of naked limbs, Rex and Gabe both with their heads on Boone's chest. Boone kissed the top of both of their heads. "Fuck, that was fantastic. I've never come so hard in my entire life." He ran his hands up and down Rex's back and kissed his head again. "I know it's a little late but in case you're wondering I'm clean."

Rex chuckled and bit Boone's nipple. "I figured you cared enough not to let me do that if you weren't." He laved the hard nub and sucked it into his mouth. Coming off with a loud pop, Rex looked into Boone's eyes. "Do you understand what's going on here?"

Boone gave him a sideways smile that showed off his dimples. "I kinda hope it means you both want me. And the way I'm feelin' right now, I hope it's for more than a one-night affair."

Gabe sat up and turned his face up to Boone. "That's exactly what it means. We both felt a connection to you that we don't wanna ignore. I know this is all new to you but I need to know whether this is just a passing kink for you or if you're feeling the same thing we are. We don't want to fall for you and get our hearts broken when you just up and leave at the end of the summer." Gabe held Rex's hand while he waited for Boone's answer.

Boone blew out a breath. "I don't know, guys. This is all so new to me. I mean…I've never shared my emotions with anyone besides Tim until yesterday. There's something about the two of you that's starting to change me. I feel a connection that I can't explain. It's just there. I'd like to explore these emotions I'm feeling right now but they're so new that I can't make you promises yet. If that's a deal breaker then I'm sorry. I have to be honest with you and I do have to finish my education."

Rex kissed Boone's chest and then blew on his nipple. "We can't ask for any more from you than honesty, Boone." Rex licked his nipple idly. "Did you always want to be a geologist?"

Boone ran his fingers through Rex's black hair. "No. I always thought I wanted to be a physical therapist. I wanted to help kids like Tim but once I'd spent a couple years in college I started visiting the facilities where I'd have to work and decided that wasn't for me. All the places were exactly the same. The same equipment. The same exercises used. It was just depressing. So…because I was really good in science I decided to move more toward geology." Gabe attached himself to Boone's other nipple and began circling it with his tongue. Boone groaned and his cock began to fill again. These two men were going to kill him.

Rex popped off Boone's nipple and began massaging his cock. "Tell us what you really wanted to do with the kids that the facilities didn't offer?" Rex had a feeling he knew and an idea began to form in his head.

Boone reached for Gabe and brought him up for a kiss. "I want you to fuck me, Gabe. I want you to fuck me while I fuck Rex."

Rex stopped his massage and smiled at him. "Answer my question first and then I'll let you stick this pole as far up my ass as you can get it."

Boone moaned. "I wanted to teach the kids to ride horses. I saw what it did for Tim and I wanted to give that to someone else. Tim always said it was like he was walking again. But most of the rehab facilities are in the city. I think there might be a few to use horses around the country but not around here."

Gabe kissed him and dug the lube out of the pocket of his jeans. "Good answer. Now it's time for an ass fuckin'." Gabe went over to Rex and shoved him to his back. He squirted some lube onto Boone's fingers and pointed. "You stretch Rex out while I get you ready."

Boone reached between Rex's legs and spread them wider. He rimmed Rex's hole with the lube and then began inserting his fingers—first one, then two and finally three. Boone looked back at Gabe, who was going to town in Boone's ass. He held out his hand and smiled. "Give me the tube. I think he's gonna need a lot more lube to take me." He smiled down at Rex and leaned in for a kiss, shoving his ass higher in the air.

Gabe bent and bit Boone's butt cheek. "Remind me to tongue-fuck you later, sexy ass." He inserted several fingers and found Boone's pleasure gland. Stroking his finger over it several times, he used his other hand to lube up his own cock. "Ready?"

Boone looked down into Rex's eyes. "You ready for me, cowboy?"

Rex hooked his arms under his knees and pulled his thighs to his chest, presenting even more of his ass. "Do your worst, darlin'."

Boone lined himself up and slowly entered Rex. He could tell that Rex was feeling the bite of pain that he felt earlier but he was already moaning so Boone figured it wasn't too painful. He pushed in an inch at a time until he was buried to the root. Boone stilled and looked over his shoulder to Gabe. "Your turn, gorgeous. Fuck me hard. I like the bite of pain that comes with a good, hard fuckin'."

Gabe smiled and shoved his cock in to the hilt. "Oh fuck, you feel good." Gabe pulled out and slammed back in. Each time he shoved Boone's cock a little farther into Rex's ass. After a short time they came up with a thrust-counterthrust motion and all three men were grunting and moaning.

The sound of balls hitting asses combined with the sound of wet cocks slamming into assholes was deafening even out in the open field. Gabe closed his eyes and just listened. It was so damned sexy he felt his balls draw up. "Can't wait...gonna come...*now*!" Gabe came so hard that his entire body shook. It felt like the top of his head had blown off.

Boone was next, cursing to the sky as he exploded into Rex. He immediately pulled out and dropped down to suck on Rex's cock. Rex thrust up into Boone's warm, sucking mouth.

Rex howled as usual and erupted down Boone's throat. "Damn, I love your mouth." He winked down at Boone. "Your cock's not half bad either, darlin'."

The three of them spread out on the blanket to get their breath and their strength back. Finally Rex sat up and reached for his saddlebag. He withdrew a rag and wiped Gabe's cock off, then he moved to Boone's ass and cock and finally his own ass and cock. When he was finished he threw the rag back in his bag and reached for his jeans. "As much as I'd love to stay here all day and fuck the both of you, I've got cattle to check on."

Rex stood up and slipped his jeans back on. He found his shirt in a pile of clothes and shrugged into it, still watching his two lovers kiss. He shook his head and got his boots on. "You guys could at least come up for air long enough to tell me goodbye."

Boone and Gabe broke apart and both stood. They reached for Rex and each gave him a tongue-lashing kiss. Rex smacked them both on the ass. "I think this new relationship is gonna work out just fine." He grabbed up his hat and strolled toward his horse. "I should be done in about three hours. I'll expect both of you to be back at the house with a hot shower and a beer ready for me." Rex gave them one last smile and rode off.

Gabe raised his eyebrow and reached for Boone again. "Who made him lord of the manor?" He wrapped his arms around Boone and fondled his ass. "You're not sorry you did this, are you?"

Boone ran his fingers through Gabe's scraggly hair. "The only thing I'm sorry about is that we didn't all find each other sooner. I feel alive again for the first time in fourteen years." He leaned in to kiss Gabe again. "Let's get dressed and go back to the house. I need to do a little work on the computer before his lordship comes home."

* * * * *

By the time Rex walked in the door dinner had been set on the table and Boone's papers neatly put into stacks on the coffee table. Rex entered the kitchen to find Boone sitting on the counter buck-naked with Gabe between his spread thighs, sucking his cock down his throat. "Damn, if that's not a beautiful sight I don't know what is." Rex walked over to the two men and pulled Gabe off Boone's cock.

He kissed first Boone and then Gabe and bent to take the long, thick cock into his mouth. He ran his tongue up the veined sides and swirled the head with his tongue. He looked over at a grinning Gabe. "Suck his sac while I swallow this monster." Gabe winked at him and Rex slid the big cock all the way down his throat. He could hear Gabe lapping at Boone's balls as he swallowed around the cock. Boone went to lie back and smacked his head against the cupboard door. Rex chuckled and the vibrations in his throat set Boone off like a rocket.

Rex swallowed as fast as he could, not wanting to miss a precious drop of Boone's cum. When he had Boone licked clean he stood and shared a kiss with each man. "Excellent appetizer, Gabe. You've really outdone yourself this time." He stepped back so Boone could jump off the counter. "So have you two done anything today beside screw around together?"

Gabe pointed his nose into the air. "I'll have you know I've been in this kitchen all afternoon slaving away and Boone's been on the laptop all day."

Rex smirked and took off his shirt. "As long as it wasn't your laptop he was working on all day. Otherwise your balls will be so sore tomorrow you won't be able to walk." He quickly kissed each man again and headed out of the kitchen. "I'm going to jump in the shower now. Give me ten minutes then I'll be ready to eat your delicious creation, Gabe."

Rex went into the bathroom and turned the shower on. He was in the middle of washing his hair when he realized it was Thursday. "Ah fuck." He'd told his mother he and Gabe would be back tonight. He wondered what he should do about Boone. Did he dare take him? His mom would be able to tell the three of them were together as soon as she saw them. Finally he decided what the hell. Rex had never kept anything of importance from Maggie so why start now.

He dried off and put clean jeans and a clean dark gray t-shirt on. He wandered back into the kitchen to find Boone and Gabe both sitting at the table waiting for him. He stopped in front of Gabe's chair and bent to kiss him then moved and did the same with Boone. Rex felt like a family already. He sat down and took a long drink of tea and cleared his throat. "Gabe, do you remember what we're supposed to do this evening? Besides fuck each other's brains out?"

Gabe looked at him, puzzled for a second, and then it dawned on him. "Maggie."

Rex nodded and dug into his chicken fried steak and mashed potatoes and gravy. He looked at Boone who looked puzzled at the mention of a woman's name. Rex swallowed. "My mother Maggie's living at the nursing home in Styler. We promised we'd visit her again tonight." Rex ran his fingers through his wet hair. "I can't believe I almost forgot."

Gabe reached across the table and squeezed his hand. "You didn't forget, Rex, so don't even think that way. Besides, I'm looking forward to it. Although I need you to make a stop at the grocery store for me on the way." Gabe glanced toward Boone, silently asking the question Rex had already asked himself.

Rex turned toward Boone and took his hand as well. "Would you please do me the honor of accompanying us to see my mother? We won't be gone more than a couple hours."

Gabe smiled at Boone. "You'll love her. She may be in a wheelchair but she's full of life and orneriness." Gabe sent Boone an unspoken signal that it was important to Rex.

Boone set down his tea and nodded. "I'd be honored to meet your mother, Rex. If the three of us stop talking and eat we can get going within a half an hour." The other two men nodded and they quickly finished their dinner.

Getting up from the table, Rex picked up his empty plate and carried it to the sink. "Good dinner, sweetheart." He began filling the sink with hot soapy water. Boone brought him some more dishes and he started washing. Gabe came up beside him and started to dry.

Boone finished clearing the table. "Hey, gorgeous, where do you keep the storage containers?"

Gabe reached over and kissed him and pointed toward the lower cabinet. "In there, but be careful, it's kind of a mess."

Rex bumped his hip against Gabe. "Are you implying I'm messy?"

Gabe reached over and cupped Rex's cock. "We all have to have one fault, baby. That's the only one I've found." He gave the cock in his hand a couple of squeezes and went back to drying.

* * * * *

They finished cleaning the kitchen and jumped into Rex's cherry red quad-cab pickup. They all decided to sit up front with Boone in the middle. They hadn't even gotten to the end of the drive before Boone's hands started wandering.

He looked out the windshield like he was bored but his hands were doing some major cock rubbing. Gabe went so far as to scoot down a little and spread his legs. Rex just shook his head but he also spread his legs a little wider. Boone continued to rub until Gabe groaned. Boone seemed to take that as a sign and unbuttoned Gabe's jeans. "Why don't either one of you wear any underwear?" he asked as Gabe's cock sprang out of his jeans.

Rex laughed and reached over to rub the bulge in Boone's jeans. "Gabe started it and I decided since it was so nice to have such easy access to his lovely cock that I'd return the favor. Believe me just that one piece of clothing makes a huge difference when it's between you and the cock you're hungry for."

Boone bent down toward Gabe's cock. "Speaking of hungry." Boone ran his tongue down the length of Gabe's cock.

Gabe grabbed a handful of honey-colored hair and thrust upward. "Yeah, honey, suck that cock."

Boone obliged and swallowed Gabe's cock. He unzipped his own pants and started stroking himself while sucking Gabe off.

Rex looked over at the two and groaned. "Oh fuck. You two are going to get us all killed. How am I supposed to drive when I've got a view like that to watch?" Rex heard that little needy sound that Gabe did just before he comes. "Get ready, Boone. Gabe's about to blow." In the next second Gabe slammed his fist against the dash and came down Boone's throat. Boone quickly cleaned Gabe up and turned to take Rex in his mouth. He barely made it before Rex pulled to the side of the road and emptied his seed into Boone's mouth as well.

Boone cleaned Rex as Gabe found and started sucking on Boone's cock in earnest. Boone sat up and watched as Gabe's head bobbed up and down on his dick until Boone couldn't take it any longer. He thrust up once and yelled Gabe's name as he came.

Two minutes later they resumed their trek to Styler, all three of them with a smile upon their sated faces. Gabe turned toward Boone and Rex. "Just so you know I probably only have one good cum left in my balls for the night. So use it wisely, my friends."

Rex started laughing as he pulled up to the grocery store. Gabe jumped out and went inside. When he came out he had a brown bag in his hand. He went to the back of Rex's truck and retrieved a metal tackle box. He climbed back in the cab and noticed the looks he was getting from Boone and Rex. "What?"

Rex looked at him and spread his hands. "Exactly what are you up to?"

Gabe chuckled and brought a box of candy bars out of the bag. "Making brownie points with Maggie. You got a problem with that?" Gabe proceeded to empty the chocolate bars into the metal box. He then withdrew a padlock and key out of the grocery bag and locked the box. He put the key on a dog tag chain he'd dug out of his pocket. "Okay, I'm ready to make some serious brownie points."

Rex laughed and shook his head as he pulled out of the parking lot. "Brownie points, hell. You're trying to put my poor sweet mom into a sugar coma."

Gabe reached around Boone and punched Rex in the arm. "Well, we'll just see who gets the bigger kiss. You for bringing Boone or me for my inventive chocolate bar safe."

They parked in the parking lot and all piled out of the truck. Gabe leaned into Boone's side. "Don't be nervous, you'll love her and she'll love you." They walked inside and went down the hall to Maggie's room.

Rex knocked on the door and then opened it. "Mom, did you remember we were coming tonight?" Rex entered the room then motioned for the others to follow. He walked over to Maggie and gave her a hug and a kiss. "How are ya, Mom?"

Maggie patted his hand. "I'm right as rain, dearest boy. I see you brought another fine-looking man with you today." She winked at Gabe and Boone. "What? Are you collecting them now?"

Rex chuckled and drew Boone closer to his side. "I guess you could say that, Mom. I'd like to introduce you to Boone Fowler. Boone, this lovely lady is my mom, Maggie Cotton."

Boone took her hand and bent down onto his knees so he could be eye level with her. "I'm very pleased to meet you, Mrs. Cotton."

Maggie raised her brow and looked up at Rex. "Another charmer, I see." She looked at Boone again and patted his hand. "Please call me Mom or Maggie. I'm way too young to be Mrs. Cotton." She looked over Boone's shoulder as he stood up. "You, young man. Why are you hidin' over there? Come over and give Momma some sugar."

Gabe smiled and walked over to Maggie. "Are you asking for a kiss or chocolate?"

Maggie giggled. "Well, both of course."

Gabe bent and kissed her cheek. He pulled a chair up to Maggie and sat down. "I come bearing gifts." He handed her the metal box. "I brought this for you to keep your valuables in. Here's a key that unlocks it and I put it on a chain so you could wear it around your neck."

Maggie took the key from him and opened the box. "Oh my. I've never seen so many chocolate bars in one place. Thank you, dear boy." She leaned over and gave him another kiss.

Gabe grinned up at Rex. "Now you can settle a bet for us. Who deserves a bigger kiss? Me for bringing you this box filled with chocolate bars or Rex for bringing Boone?" Gabe waited while she seemed to be really thinking about it.

Finally Maggie sighed and patted Gabe's hand. "Well, while I love the chocolate and the box the chocolate will only last for so long. Whereas the gift that Rex brought I have a feeling will be around a lot longer. So I'd have to go with Rex's gift of another son." She patted Gabe's hand. "Please don't take it too hard, Gabe. I have a feeling you're a winner too."

All three men looked at each other. Rex bent to kiss his mom's head. "How did you get to be so wise, Mom?"

She leaned in closer to Rex and stage-whispered. "Don't tell anyone but I'm an old woman. It's our job to be wise. Besides the three of you have love and lust written all over your faces. Now get on home and enjoy each other and leave me to my chocolate."

Gabe kissed Maggie one more time. "Remember, Mag...Mom, only one a day. Rex is afraid I'm trying to put you into a sugar coma." He laughed and stepped back.

"Thank you for the gift, dearest son." She pointed toward Boone. "I don't believe you've given me a kiss yet, young man."

Boone bent and kissed her cheek and blushed while doing it. "Thank you for being so tolerant, Maggie."

Rex bent and kissed her cheek. "I love you, Mom, and we'll see you in a couple of days."

Chapter Eight

Two weeks later

ဢ

Returning from Styler, Boone appeared lost in thought. They were on their way home from yet another visit to Maggie. Boone and Gabe had both insisted on seeing her every couple days. He ran his hand up and down Rex's thigh. He wasn't getting frisky, he was just thinking. "Hey, Rex? Why doesn't your mom live with you? I mean, beside the wheelchair she seems to be in good health."

Rex reached down and squeezed Boone's hand. "Gabe and I talked about it but my house isn't wheelchair accessible. We thought that we would try to figure out our money situation and maybe eventually build her a little house on the ranch that's wheelchair accessible." He shrugged. "That may be a few years down the road though. Although I hate to see her in that nursing home, I just don't have anything else for her right now. At least it's close enough we can get in every couple of days to see her."

Boone was silent the rest of the way home. When they pulled up to the house he turned to Rex. "I'm going to say something and I want you to let me finish before you say anything, all right?"

Rex put his arm around him. "Sure, darlin', what's on your mind?" He worriedly looked past Boone to Gabe.

Gabe cleared his throat and opened his door. "As much as I know you want to get whatever it is off your chest, Boone, could we go in to the living room? It's damn hot out here and I could use a beer." Gabe waited for Boone's nod and got out of the truck.

They walked into the living room, only stopping long enough to grab a beer out of the fridge, and sat down on one of the couches. Rex opened his beer and took a long pull then set it down and wrapped his arms around Boone. "Okay, tell me what's wrong."

Boone leaned in and kissed Rex. "Nothing's wrong, Rex. That's one of the things I wanted to say. In the two weeks I've been here I feel closer to the two of you than I have to anyone except Tim. And that leads to what I'm going to ask next." Boone took a deep breath and exhaled. "I want you to let me pay to have a house built for your mom."

Boone could see the rejection to his offer written on Rex's face. He held his hand up. "Let me finish. I told you my father kicked me out of his life when I was seventeen but what I didn't tell you is that he died two years ago in a ranch accident. He never had his will changed and I inherited a very large, very prosperous cattle ranch that I've never even been back to. I'd like to do something good with some of the money my father left behind. I was too young to do everything I wanted to do for Tim but I'm more than financially able to do this for the only people left in this world that I care about. At least tell me you'll think about it, Rex? If it's a matter of pride with you I'll let you pay me back when we bring oil up that well."

Gabe and Rex both dropped their jaws. Gabe took Boone's hand. "Are you saying you think there's oil here?"

Boone smiled and kissed Gabe. "What I believe is that the first geologist was right but his figures were wrong. I'd say the oil is another ten thousand feet down. The only problem I see is it will be a very expensive undertaking. There's no guarantee as to how much oil is actually down there. I think the two of you need to decide what you're willing to risk and exactly how much money it is that you need to make you happy."

Rex looked sideways at Boone and narrowed his eyes. "What are you trying to say, Boone? You know more about this than either one of us. If you've got suggestions or opinions please share them."

Boone took his hat off and threw it on the table. "All I'm saying is that you have a nice home here. If you decide to search for the oil you could bankrupt yourselves and lose what you already have. I guess what I'm trying to understand is what exactly do you want with the money from the oil that the two of you don't already possess? If it's a house for your mom let me do it for her and you. If it's to burn down the main house fine let's do it. All we have to do is call the fire department and let them practice on it. You both need to decide what it is you want and then weigh the risk of losing the ranch against it."

Gabe slowly nodded his head. "Let me understand this. You believe there is in fact oil on my land but you think it's too expensive for us to get it out?"

Boone closed his eyes and nodded. "Yes and no. I can almost guarantee that there's some oil on your ranch. The problem is until you spend a huge amount of money, which I'm guessing neither one of you have, you won't really know how much oil is down there. I think you would be better off approaching an investment group and leasing the mineral rights of a certain section or percentage of your land."

Rex rubbed Boone's back. He could tell Boone was starting to get a little frustrated with the two of them but Boone needed to understand how new this all was to them. "I'm really not trying to sound stupid, Boone, but what does it mean to lease the mineral rights of a piece of land?"

Boone leaned over and kissed him. "Basically, an oil company would lease everything under the surface of your land. Normally they would pay you an upfront amount and then a percentage of the oil profit. The lease is usually written up so that the oil company holds the lease until the well is no longer productive. Which in this case could be five years or one hundred years. The thing to keep in mind is that they will have the right to put as many oil wells in that leased ground as they deem worthy to get to their property underneath the ground. That's why I suggest leasing only fifty to one hundred acres. Your cattle can still be on the property but the risk is yours should they get hurt. The oil company would also have the right to either put in a road or just drive through your land in order to get to their wells. It's a lot to think about but your income could increase nicely without having to risk anything you already have. Can I ask one more question?" At Gabe's nod Boone went on. "Why were you interested in finding oil in the first place?"

Gabe looked at Rex and shrugged. "Water. My cattle need water that we don't have. I just sold off half my herd because I didn't have enough water."

Boone smiled and kissed him. "I think you should lease the mineral rights and I can find the water for you. I'm not a hydrologist but I think I can find more water for you. Use the money you get for the lease to find more water. Then you not only have the water you desperately need but you get a yearly percentage check from the oil company."

Rex reached out and tackled Boone down on the couch. He kissed him deeply. "I knew there was a reason you were meant to come here besides being our soul mate." He kissed him again. "Let's go to bed. Too much technical talk has totally deflated my cock."

Gabe laughed but agreed. "Come to the bedroom and we'll see how permanent that condition is." Gabe got up and locked up the house. He found Rex and Boone already in the bedroom stripping each other. Gabe took his own clothes off but continued to watch the scene before him.

They got each other's clothes off and started softly touching each other, exploring each other's bodies. Rex ran his fingers over Boone's face, touching his eyes, cheekbones, the length of his nose and mouth. He leaned in and ran his tongue around the perfect outline of Boone's mouth. Gabe saw Boone shiver under Rex's touch. Rex licked his way down Boone's neck and bit lightly. Gabe smiled. He knew how much Rex liked to bite.

Smoothly Gabe walked across the room to the little chair in the corner. He sat and spread his thighs. As he watched his two lovers touch each other's bodies he began stroking his own rampant hard-on.

Rex made his way to Boone's smoothly muscled chest. He began scraping the bronzed skin with his teeth. He circled Boone's areola with his tongue and teeth, flicking the little bronzed nub and then biting it. Boone moaned and put his hands into Rex's hair. Gabe didn't know if he was merely holding on or if he was now directing the show. Rex latched on to the nipple, from the hollowing of his cheeks Gabe would say he was sucking hard.

Boone's "holy fuck" reverberated through the room. Gabe started working his cock a little faster, a little harder. Boone must have seen movement out of the corner of his eye because he looked straight at Gabe and held out his hand. Gabe shook his head. "I want to watch the two of you. I'll join you later."

Rex didn't even raise his head off Boone's chest. Boone pulled him off his nipple and subtly pushed his shoulder downward. Rex relented and moved his ministrations south. He ran his tongue along the ridges of Boone's six-pack and into the depths of his belly button.

Gabe ran his hand over the end of his cock and gathered the moisture that was beginning to collect and used it as lube to aid his stroking. He leaned back in the chair even farther when Rex reached Boone's huge cock. Gabe could see Rex's pink tongue snake out and run up the length of Boone's cock, paying special attention to the veins and ridges. Rex looked up into Boone's eyes as he dipped his tongue into the slit to gather some of his essence. Boone groaned and pushed his cock toward Rex's face. It was obvious to Gabe what Boone was after.

He was rewarded when Rex smiled up at him and swallowed the entire length of his cock. Damn, how did he do that? The sight was so damn erotic that Gabe knew he wanted a piece of that ass. Boone's ass was hollowed in at the sides and Gabe's mouth watered just looking at him. He rose from his chair and knelt behind Boone. He took a white globe in each hand and separated them. Boone moaned again louder this time under the twin assaults.

Gabe ran his tongue up the crack of Boone's ass. He stuck his thumbs in the tight puckered hole and made room for his tongue. Gabe thrust his tongue in and out of his hole as Boone thrust his cock in and out of Rex's mouth. Gabe could tell Boone was getting close when his asshole clamped down around his thumbs and tongue. Boone growled and began pumping faster.

"Yeah, eat that cock." Boone reached back to grab Gabe's hair. "Fuck, Gabe, that feels good. Love your tongue."

Gabe replaced his thumbs with his longer fingers so he could fill Boone even more. Boone's ass almost pinched his tongue off when he shot down Rex's throat, screaming their names as he did. They all fell to the bed.

Gabe ran his hands up Rex's thigh until he found the ultimate prize. Rex was so turned on, his cock was leaking like a sieve. Gabe leaned over and ran his tongue around inside Rex's open mouth. "I love you, baby." He leaned over Rex to get to a still-recovering Boone. He kissed him passionately. "I love you, honey."

Boone went still. Gabe looked at Rex afraid he'd pushed too hard too fast. Gabe and Rex waited with bated breath for Boone's reaction to his declaration.

Boone didn't keep them waiting for long. He grabbed the back of Gabe's head and hauled him on top of him. He pulled Gabe's face up to his and practically gave him a tonsillectomy. Boone pulled back and looked into Gabe's light gray eyes. "I don't understand how it's even possible but I love you too." He ate Gabe's mouth a little more and then turned to pull Rex up to join in their kiss.

Rex licked at both Gabe's and Boone's mouths and reached for Gabe's cock. Boone kissed Rex's nose in a loving gesture. "I love you too, cowboy."

Rex groaned and snuggled in even closer. "I love you, darlin'. Now...who's gonna fuck me because I really need it?"

* * * * *

Boone was up early the next morning working at the kitchen table on his laptop. Gabe had gone to check water and hay in the pastures and Rex was fixing fences. Boone was searching for gas and oil companies operating in the area that might be interested in securing the mineral rights to one hundred acres of the ranch. Gabe told him the ranch was a little over a thousand acres so leasing one hundred wouldn't be a hardship if they could find more water somewhere.

Boone knew the transaction would all go a lot easier if they used a broker but then you had to share in the profits. He thought that with his master's degree in geology he could convince the oil company he knew what he was talking about. He knew he needed to get into town and make copies of the file and the maps of the ranch.

He got sidetracked and began thinking about Maggie. Boone knew Rex was a proud man but he had to convince him to let Boone help with building her a home. He pulled up the still-untouched bank account for the Flying Duchess, the ranch he now owned. The Duchess had increased in value since he'd last looked into it. The prosperous ranch, including the house, acreage and cattle was worth millions of dollars. Without giving it much thought, Boone sent off an email to a local realtor in Houston and asked him to list the ranch for sale—lock, stock and barrel. It was time he put the past behind him and moved on with his life.

Boone searched for building plans. Although Rex hadn't agreed to let him build a house for Maggie, Boone wanted to be prepared for the argument that was sure to come. He found a log cabin kit online. "Perfect," Boone mumbled to himself.

The kit included all the materials needed to build a small one-bedroom log cabin. Boone would have to see if the company did special orders because Maggie would need wider doorways and a new bathroom designed for handicapped accessibility but other than that it would be perfect.

He saved the website to his list of favorites and went back to searching for oil companies. Boone found a couple and sent off letters of inquiry via email. He closed down the laptop and looked at the maps in front of him. These maps would help in finding water but Boone bet there were other maps in the main house that would be better. He scratched a quick note telling the guys they could find him at the main house and why and left.

* * * * *

Boone walked into the house and wasted no time going down to the basement. He went to the storage room that Rex had shown him two weeks ago. Wow, had it only been two weeks ago that he met these two men? He found the box in the back corner but the light didn't quite reach it. He looked around for someplace to move the box, but the room was truly crammed full of other boxes. Besides the fact that the large wooden box weighed a ton. Boone put his hands on his hips. He needed more light. He decided to go upstairs and look for something he could use.

He found a kerosene lamp in the kitchen along with a box of matches and took them downstairs. He knew a flashlight would have been better but then he'd have to hold it. Boone lit the lamp and set it on top of the stacked boxes. He pulled out one and then another of the maps. He was sure he'd seen a hydrology map a couple weeks ago.

Boone pulled out another rolled map and inadvertently bumped into the stack of boxes holding the lantern. Boone saw the lantern wobble and tip over in slow motion. He reached toward it but knew it was too late. He jumped back quickly, knowing the spilling kerosene would ignite quickly and looked around for a blanket or tarp to smother the flames. The boxes of old papers ignited quickly and Boone suddenly remembered the room Rex had pointed out that Buck held Jenny captive in. He ran out of the storage room and to the tiny room. He grabbed the quilt off the bed and ran some cold water over it from the nearby sink.

Boone raced back to the storage room but as soon as he tried using the blanket he could see it was a lost cause. There was just too much stuff just waiting to burn. He ripped off a piece from the blanket and held it over his mouth while he tried in vain to drag some of the flammable boxes out into the empty hall. If he could just get rid of some of the fuel for the fire he might have a chance. He quickly carried and pulled about ten boxes out before he realized it was no use. He decided to just get the hell out of there.

Boone turned and ran toward the stairs. The smoke was getting thicker all the time. He felt his way to the stairs and tried to take them two at a time in his haste to leave the burning house. He missed a step and tripped. Boone's head cracked against one of the heavy wooden treads and his world went black.

When he came to, the fire was already down the hall and the smoke was overwhelming. He felt his head, his hand came away wet and sticky but he didn't have time to dwell on it. He managed to crawl up the stairs and out to the porch before the blow to his head and the amount of smoke in his lungs became too much. The last thing he remembered was calling out for Gabe and Rex.

* * * * *

Rex was riding back to the barn on Chief when he saw the smoke. He punched his heels into Chief's flanks and took off for home. The closer he got, the more he could see that it was the main house that was on fire and not his house or the barn. He pulled Chief up to his house so he could run in and call the fire department. Rex ran into the kitchen, grabbed the phone and called 9-1-1. The operator answered and Rex began to give her the address and details of the fire. He spotted the note on the table as the operator told him the fire department was on their way. Rex quickly read the note and told the dispatcher to send an ambulance. Rex dropped the phone and raced toward the main house.

He could see Boone, facedown, sprawled out on the porch with his feet still inside the burning house. Rex didn't think his legs would carry him fast enough. He took the stairs three at a time and reached Boone before the fire did. He didn't know what was wrong with Boone until he turned him over to carry him to safety. A long bloody gash on his forehead told him what he needed to know. Rex lifted Boone's body and ran down the stairs all the way to the shaded front of the barn.

He laid him down and raced back to his house. He was just getting cool water and a rag when he heard Lolly race up to the house. Rex grabbed a bottle of water and ran outside. "Boone's hurt. He's by the barn." Gabe raced Lolly to the barn with Rex running as fast as he could behind him. Rex saw Gabe jump off Lolly and kneel at Boone's side.

Rex knelt on the other side of Boone and began pouring water on his forehead so he could assess the damage. The cut was deep and already starting to swell. Rex looked up at Gabe. "I told the dispatcher to send an ambulance when I saw the note from Boone. He was in the main house looking for the hydrology map. They should be here any second." Just then the high-pitched sounds of sirens filled the air.

Gabe lay down beside Boone and cradled him in his arms. He kissed his soft unresponsive lips. "Boone? Honey, wake up for me. I love you. You have to open your eyes, honey."

The ambulance pulled up to the group of men while the fire trucks surrounded the burning house. The technicians gently moved both Rex and Gabe out of the way as they worked on Boone. They started an IV and turned to Rex. "I see the cut on his head but do you know how long he was in the building before he got out?"

Rex pulled Gabe to his side. "No, he was passed out on the porch. Half in, half out when I found him about ten or fifteen minutes ago. I tried to wash some of the blood off his head but it just keeps coming."

The technician nodded. "Head wounds tend to do that. We'll take him in to the hospital. I'm figuring he's suffered not only a concussion but smoke inhalation as well. Are you going to follow us or come later after you check on the condition of your house?"

"Fuck the house. No one lives in it anyway. We'll follow you as soon as I talk with the fire captain." They loaded Boone into the ambulance and took off in a cloud of dust. Rex and Gabe ran to the truck and got in. They stopped long enough for Rex to have a quick word with the fire captain then took off toward the hospital in Styler.

Chapter Nine

On the way to the hospital Rex noticed that Gabe seemed a little too calm. Rex didn't know what was going on inside him but he thought Gabe might be in shock. He reached over and took Gabe's hand. Gabe didn't even look at him. Rex licked his lips and cleared his throat. "I told the fire captain not to risk anyone's life trying to save the house. If it burns it burns. Just as long as the fire doesn't spread to anything else."

Gabe nodded but said nothing. He continued to look out the window. He was really starting to worry Rex. Rex made a quick decision and pulled off the road. He cut off the engine and pulled Gabe into his arms. He kissed the top of his head. "He's going to be all right, sweetheart. They'll get him into the hospital and stitch him up and put him on oxygen for a while and he'll be good as new."

Gabe finally turned to face Rex. "I knew it was too good to be true. I've gone my whole life with no one to love and in three weeks' time I have three people whom I love more than my own life. I knew I was getting greedy and now God's punishing me for it."

Rex closed his eyes at the pain he heard in Gabe's voice. He wrapped him up a little tighter and kissed his soft lips. "No, sweetheart. God isn't punishing you. It was just an accident. Accidents happen and it's no one's fault. Boone'll be fine. He'll be back home with us before you know it. He needs us as much as we need him. He's not going anywhere. Give me a kiss and let's get to the hospital to be with our man."

Gabe nodded his head and wrapped his arms around Rex's neck and kissed him so hard and with so much passion that it split Rex's lip just a bit. Gabe must have tasted the blood because he stopped the kiss and drew back. "I'm sorry about that, Rex. I'm just so afraid of losing what I've spent a lifetime looking for."

Rex licked the blood from his lip and kissed him again. "You're not about to lose anything, sweetheart. Boone and I love you. You've even got my mom under your spell." At Gabe's slight nod Rex started the truck and took off toward the hospital once again.

They reached the emergency room and parked the truck. Side by side they ran into the emergency room and found the information nurse. Rex stepped up and knocked on the glass partition. "Excuse me, ma'am, but they just brought our friend in with a cut and possible smoke inhalation. Could you tell us where he is?"

The nurse smiled, "Please have a seat and when they're done working on him someone will be out to speak with you."

Rex nodded and thanked her. He led Gabe over to the waiting room. Gabe was still a little too quiet for his peace of mind so he decided to engage him in a discussion to get his mind off Boone. "Tell me what your thoughts are regarding the oil well."

Gabe looked over at him like he was crazy. It finally dawned on him what Rex was trying to do. He decided to play along for a while. "I think we should do whatever Boone thinks would be best. I think he cares enough about us to have our best interests in mind. I don't care anything about becoming rich, Rex. I just want a home filled with people I love and a satisfying way to make a living."

Rex smiled. Gabe was playing right into his plan for the future. "What kind of work would you consider satisfying?"

Gabe shrugged his shoulders and leaned back in the chair. "I'd like to do something outside where I can use both my brain and my hands. Something that allows me to be my own boss."

"What would you think about opening some sort of riding facility for the handicapped? That way we could put the ranch to good use and still work outside. Boone could set up the programs and we could help with the children."

Gabe looked at him sideways. "What about the cattle? We'd still need them to make a living because I'd rather do the riding therapy as a nonprofit kind of thing. I could never live with myself if I knew I was making a profit off handicapped people."

Despite being surrounded by people in the waiting room, Rex leaned over and gave Gabe a quick kiss. "That's why I love you so much. You've got a good and honest heart. Okay, we'd have to keep the cattle but if Boone can find us more water then at least it should be easier. Plus we'd still have a little money coming in from the oil well. I think we could do it."

Gabe rubbed his jaw. "I think I'd like to talk to Ben about it. He confided in me one time when we were in the jungle that he's a millionaire. No one else on the team knows and he made me promise not to tell anyone. I know for a fact that all his money is just sitting in a bank. He feels like its dirty money because of what his mother did to herself and him to get it. I think he might relish the opportunity to do something good with it, like helping to fund a riding program for the handicapped. We don't even need to stick with just kids and with all of the added improvements to the ranch Mom could get around a lot more easily."

Rex looked at him and smiled. "Do you realize you just unconsciously called Maggie Mom? We'll have to talk to Boone about everything that would have to be done to the ranch in order for it to become wheelchair friendly." He squeezed Gabe's hand. "I don't know about you but I'm excited already."

They sat in the waiting room for another hour before a doctor came to speak with them. He said they had to put thirty stitches in Boone's forehead but they'd called down a plastic surgeon to do it. Boone was awake and alert but he did have a pretty good concussion and they would need to keep him overnight. The doctor went on to tell them that the smoke inhalation wasn't that severe. They had him on oxygen but said he would be fine by morning.

They moved Boone to a private room and Rex and Gabe finally got to go in to see him. Rex reached him first and bent to kiss his cheek. He was careful not to dislodge the oxygen tube in Boone's nose but Boone was having none of it. He ripped the tube out of his nose and pulled Rex down for a deep kiss. "That's more like it." Boone turned to face Gabe. "C'mere, you're next."

Gabe stepped up to the bed and received his own mind-blowing kiss. Gabe licked Boone's lips. "I love you, honey. I'm glad you're gonna be all right." He picked up the oxygen tube and put it back into Boone's nostrils. "Wear that so you can get better and come home where you belong."

Rex took Boone's hand. "We've got a lot of plans for you, darlin'. Some of them outside the bedroom even." He winked and squeezed Boone's hand. "The doctor told us they're keeping you for the night but I'm going to try to persuade him that we can take good care of you at home. As a matter of fact I'm going to go look for him right now." Rex kissed Boone's hand and walked out the door.

Boone looked at Gabe. Gabe shrugged his shoulders. "Our house won't be a home without you in it. Even for one night. We need you just as much as we need each other." Gabe pulled up a chair and sat by Boone's bed.

Boone took his hand. "I'm sorry about the house." Boone's voice sounded scratchy and sore. Gabe handed him a glass of water. Boone took a couple sips and continued. "I know you hated it but it was still yours. I hope it didn't have any paperwork inside that you'll need." Boone closed his eyes and blew out a breath.

"It was my fault. I was looking for the hydrology map and the corner of the basement was too dark. So stupid me got a kerosene lamp and set it on top of some boxes so I could see. I turned around and hit the stack of boxes and the lamp fell over. I tried to put it out with a wet blanket." He stopped to catch his breath and took a sip of water.

"When I saw that wasn't going to work I started carrying boxes out of the storage room." At Gabe's narrowing eyes Boone shrugged. "I know. I wasn't thinking right. I just couldn't believe I'd caught your house on fire. Finally when I saw it was useless I tried to run up the stairs but the smoke was so thick I missed a tread and smacked my head. I must have blacked out for a couple of minutes but when I came to I managed to crawl up the steps and out to the fresh air of the porch." Tears started falling down Boone's cheeks from underneath his long blond lashes.

Gabe leaned over him and kissed the tears away. "The house doesn't matter to me at all, Boone. You do. Besides, look at it this way. Now I'll get an insurance check for a house I hated. Maybe we can build a new one with the money and refit Rex's for Maggie."

Boone opened his tear-filled eyes. "You really still want me around?"

Gabe ran his fingers through Boone's tangled mass of blond hair. "Want you around? Boone, haven't you understood anything Rex and I have been saying to you? We want you to grow old with us. This isn't just an affair for either one of us, Boone. That's why I told you before that you need to be sure of what you're doing with us. Because we're playing for keeps."

Boone tore the oxygen out of his nose again. He held his arms out to Gabe. "Hold me, Gabe. Tell me you love me one more time and I'll believe you."

Gabe wiped Boone's tears and kissed him. "I love you, Boone. Please be a part of our family forever."

Boone kissed him back. "Even with this ugly scar I'm going to have, you still want me?"

Gabe softly fingered the white bandage. "It will give you more of a roguish appearance. You'll be even sexier when it heals."

Boone held Gabe tight to his chest. "Families don't have my money and your money and Rex's money. They have our money. It's the only way I'll agree to stay. I want us all to be equal."

Gabe heard Rex's voice coming down the hall. He looked toward the door expectantly. "I'll have to discuss it with Rex."

Rex came through the door with the doctor. The doctor listened to Boone's lungs and checked his pupils. He smiled at Boone and pointed toward Rex. "This gentleman has assured me that he could take care of you better at home so I'm going to release you into his care. If you start feeling nauseous or dizzy call my answering service. You'll need to make an office appointment to see me in two days and then again in ten days to have your stitches removed. Do you have any questions?"

Rex asked the doctor general questions regarding diet and wound care. When he finished, all three thanked the doctor. Gabe went to the armoire and retrieved the plastic bag containing Boone's clothes. He started to open the bag and then changed his mind.

"I'm going to run down the street while you two are waiting for the paperwork to go through." Gabe held up the plastic bag. "I think these clothes will need to be thrown away. The smell through the plastic is enough to make me sick. I'll run down to the store and pick up a pair of sweats and a t-shirt." Rex nodded and Gabe left to run his errand.

When he got back about fifteen minutes later Boone was just signing the release papers. Gabe handed him the shopping bag. Sweats, t-shirt and flip-flops. Gabe grinned to himself as Boone started to put the clothes on. Not only had he purposely forgotten the underwear but he got him a size smaller than he usually wore in the sweatpants. The result was fantastic. Boone's thick cock was outlined beautifully in the black sweatpants. Gabe couldn't help it. He released a little sigh and adjusted his cock in his confining jeans.

Boone looked down at his pants and then at Gabe. "Are you trying to get me arrested, gorgeous?" Boone pulled the t-shirt over his head and pulled it down as far as he could. The result saved poor Boone's modesty.

Gabe stuck out his bottom lip. "Damn, Boone. I like the view you're trying to hide."

Boone chuckled and picked up the plastic bag. He slipped on the flip-flops and waited for the nurse to bring in the wheelchair that was hospital policy. He looked over his shoulder at Gabe and winked. "I'll pull my shirt up once we get into the truck for you, Gabe. No sense giving all these nurses a show of what they can't have, is there?"

Gabe smiled and squeezed Boone's ass. "No one can have you except me and Rex. And we do plan to have you."

Chapter Ten

ꟾ

The nurse came for Boone and wheeled him out of the hospital to where Rex was waiting with the truck. Rex came around and opened the back door. "I figured you'd like to spread out in the backseat on the way home."

Boone stood up and thanked the nurse. She pushed the wheelchair back into the hospital. Boone turned around to face Rex. "What I really want is to sit up front between the two of you."

Rex looked over at Gabe and at his nod of approval he closed the back door and opened the front passenger door. Rex helped Boone in and went around to the driver's side. Gabe hopped in beside Boone. Rex pulled out and on to the main street. He pulled up in front of a pharmacy and turned off the ignition. "I'll be right back. I need to get Boone's pain medicine and some more gauze and tape for his head."

Gabe hollered out the window as he started to go into the store. "Get a shower cap so he can keep the gauze dry and still shower." Rex nodded and entered the store.

Gabe looked over at Boone. Poor Boone looked like he wanted to curl up and go to sleep. He slipped his arm around Boone and pulled his head down to his shoulder. "Go to sleep, honey. I'll wake you when we get home."

Boone didn't put up a fight. He just snuggled in and immediately fell asleep on Gabe's shoulder.

When Rex opened the door Gabe put his fingers to his lips and Rex got into the truck and quietly shut the door. He threw the pharmacy bag onto the backseat and pulled out of the parking spot.

When they pulled into the ranch yard there was nothing left of the house. The fire captain and one of the fire trucks were still there watching for hot spots. Rex waved as he went by. He pulled up to the porch and turned off the truck. He got out and went around and opened Gabe's door.

Gabe got out and reached back in for the still-sleeping Boone. "I'm going to carry him in and put him on the couch. Then I'm gonna go talk to the fire captain. Boone explained to me how the fire started. I'm sure the captain needs to know for his reports."

Gabe cradled Boone in his arms like he weighed nothing. Even though Boone was a good-sized man he was no match for Gabe's powerful muscles. Gabe motioned toward the backseat. "Can you bring in that bag please?"

Rex reached in the backseat and grabbed the bag. He followed Gabe up the porch steps and opened the door for him. Gabe put Boone down on the sofa. He turned back toward Rex. "I shouldn't be gone long. Take care of him." He gave Rex a quick kiss and left the house.

Gabe took off toward the main house or what was left of the main house. Gabe waved to the captain and introduced himself. "I'm sorry we didn't get a chance to meet before. I'm Gabe Whitlock, the owner of the ranch."

The fire captain shook his hand. "Nice to meet you, Gabe. I'm Harley." The captain turned and motioned to the house. "Sorry about your house, we couldn't save it, but we'll make sure the fire is truly out before we leave. We don't want it to reignite in these dry conditions. I haven't got a chance to go over the ashes to find a cause yet, though."

Gabe shook his head. "I talked to Boone Fowler, who was in the house at the time, and he explained what happened." Gabe went on to tell Harley how the fire got started.

When he was finished the fire captain nodded. "I'll write it up as accidental. You should get your copy of the report by next week for the insurance company." They shook hands and the fire captain left in his SUV. One fire truck would stay for a while longer to watch the embers burn themselves out.

Gabe opened the front door quietly and found Boone sound asleep on the couch. He looked over into the kitchen and spotted Rex at the stove. He quietly shut the front door and walked into the kitchen.

Rex spotted him coming. He turned off the burner and met Gabe halfway. He opened his arms and Gabe went right into them. Their mouths met in a frenzied kiss while their hands roamed each other's bodies. With the stress of the day finally behind them they needed to touch each other.

Rex pulled Gabe's t-shirt off and attached himself to Gabe's nipple while Gabe toed off his boots. When his boots were off, he unbuttoned his jeans and pushed them down. Stepping out of his jeans he went to work on Rex's jeans. Rex must have really needed this because not only did he already have his shirt off but Gabe noticed the top button of his jeans were undone as well. Gabe raised an eyebrow and pulled Rex's jeans the rest of the way off. "Why were your pants unbuttoned? Please don't tell me you had your way with Boone already?"

Rex laughed and bit down a little harder on Gabe's nipple. Then he fell to his knees in front of Gabe and swiped his tongue against the head of Gabe's erection. "No, I didn't have my way with him but, damn, those sweats are sexy. Good job on picking those out. I think those will have to be his permanent in-house uniform from now on. The way the pants mold to his cock makes my mouth water. Speaking of cocks, how about if you sit down on the table and let me make a meal out of yours? I'm too damn old to be kneeling on this hardwood floor."

Gabe laughed and climbed up on the table. He spread his thighs as wide as he could and let them drop over the end of the table. "Dinner is served." He said with a wink.

Rex rubbed his hands together greedily. He pulled up a kitchen chair and scooted Gabe a little farther down toward the end of the table. When Gabe's erection was a mere inch from his face Rex sighed. "I love this cock." He bent his head and suckled the head with his lips and then worked his tongue down the length of Gabe's cock to his balls. He swirled the sac in his mouth and lightly sucked and nibbled.

Gabe moaned and put his feet up on the end of the table so he could have leverage to thrust upward. "Feels good, baby."

The new position gave Rex access to Gabe's ass. He continued fondling and licking Gabe's balls then moved his tongue down behind to his hole. Rex ran his tongue around the tight puckered skin and began lubing him up with his own spit. Finally he stood and spit into his hand. He rubbed the spit onto his cock and lined up with Gabe's hole. "Gonna fuck you now, sweetheart. Better hold on. I've got a feeling this table may just walk across the floor."

Gabe grabbed the edges of the table and thrust his hips toward Rex, impaling himself on Rex's cock. "Oh…yeah…fuck me, baby… Damn, you feel good."

Rex started pounding into Gabe's ass, his balls slapping Gabe's at every thrust. Just as predicted, every time Rex thrust inside Gabe, the table scooted a little bit more. When the table wedged itself against the wall Rex started fucking Gabe harder and faster. He bent down and bit the tendon in Gabe's neck as Gabe cried out his release. The tightening of Gabe's asshole milked the cum right out of Rex's cock.

Rex grunted and shook. Fuck, it felt like Gabe's ass was sucking the life out of him. Rex collapsed down onto the floor and put his head on Gabe's calf. "So good, sweetheart. It just keeps getting better and better."

Gabe rose up to look at Rex. "What are you cooking? Smells like soup."

Rex stood and got a washcloth out of the dryer and wet it with warm water. He brought it over to Gabe and began cleaning him up. When he was done he cleaned himself up and slipped his jeans back on. "I thought Boone might be hungry so I made some vegetable soup. I made three of those big cans so there should be enough for all of us. I thought I'd make you and me a sandwich also."

Gabe looked toward the living room. "Speaking of Boone, how did he manage to sleep through that?" Gabe walked into the living room and found Boone sound asleep but something was different. He laughed and went back into the kitchen. "Hey, baby…come in here and look at Boone."

Rex followed Gabe back into the living room. Gabe had to cover his mouth so he didn't laugh out loud. Rex looked down at Boone. Evidently he must have heard them fucking in the kitchen because he had his sweats pulled down below his balls and his now-limp cock in his hand. Cum was splattered all the way up his chest. Rex shook his head and went back into the kitchen and rinsed out the washcloth. He cleaned Boone with the warm washcloth and pulled Boone's cock out of his hand. Rex bent and gave the now-limp cock a sweet little kiss and then pulled the sweats back up around his waist.

Gabe and Rex went back into the kitchen. "How long should we let him sleep?"

Rex looked at the clock. "Well, it's five o'clock now and we got home a little after four so I'd say maybe until six o'clock then we can wake him and make him eat something. He needs to take his medicine with food so don't let me forget."

Gabe leaned into his arms. "You won't forget. You're very good at taking care of people. Both in the bedroom and out." Gabe drew in a deep breath. "Our poor baby is also in need of a bath. It smells like he's been sitting by a campfire all day."

Rex smiled, smelling the smoke that clung to Boone. "Maybe he should wake up sooner than six." Both men sat down on the coffee table to admire Boone's beautiful face as he slept. Rex took Gabe's hand. "When should we tell him about our surprise?"

"We should tell him after dinner and after he's been bathed. I want him naked in our bed when we talk to him about our future." Gabe couldn't resist the temptation in front of him. He reached his hand out and outlined the large cock sheathed in the tight black sweats. "I do love these sweats." He looked over and winked at Rex. "And what's inside them."

Rex stuck his hand between Gabe's jean-clad thighs and found the evidence of his desire. He rubbed the bulging material and leaned in to kiss him. He thrust his tongue into Gabe's mouth and moaned. "Damn, sweetheart. I can't get enough. It's like my cock has traveled back in time and I'm a teenager again."

Gabe kept one hand on Boone's semi-hard cock and placed the other on Rex's arousal. He leaned in for an even deeper kiss. "I love you, baby." He squeezed Rex's cock through the soft faded material of his jeans.

Boone moaned and thrust up into Gabe's hand. "If you two are going to start again at least let me join in this time."

Rex groaned and released Gabe's cock. He bent and gave Boone a kiss. "Sorry about what happened earlier. We had a lot of stress to relieve. We're glad you're home and all right, darlin'."

Gabe leaned down and kissed Boone. "We are going to feed you some dinner and then I'm sorry to tell you this but you need a bath. Afterward we can go to bed. Rex and I want to play with you but we need to talk with you too."

Boone's eyebrow rose. "Sounds serious. Have I done something to make you mad?"

Rex looked from his swollen dick to Gabe's still-swollen dick. "Does it look like we're upset with you in any way?" He leaned down to kiss Boone again. "Not bad talk, darlin', just serious, future kind of talk. I'll go turn the stove back on and make up a couple of sandwiches." Rex got up and headed for the kitchen. He stopped and looked over his shoulder. "Gabe, keep your hands off the man's cock. He needs food, medicine and a bath before playtime."

* * * * *

After dinner Rex filled the large garden tub with hot water and a little splash of citrus-scented oil while Gabe undressed Boone. Gabe pulled off his t-shirt while Rex got down on his knees to remove the tight sweats. He chewed on the bulge springing up in the sweats. "Damn. I do love these pants. The only thing better would be something tight and silky. Maybe I'll have to do some online shopping for the three of us."

They helped Boone into the water and knelt down beside the tub. Boone looked at the two men and shook his head. "No way I'm being bathed by you two unless you're naked and in here with me." He crossed his arms and stuck out his bottom lip in a mock pout.

"Damn. Isn't our man just the cutest thing when he pouts, Gabe? I say we give the man what he wants. After all it's been a really lousy day for him." Rex stood and stripped off the only thing he was wearing, his jeans. His hard as hell cock sprang up to greet Boone. It was at the perfect level and Boone put the crown of Rex's cock into his mouth and gave him one good hard suck before he popped off it and signaled for Gabe.

Gabe unbuttoned his jeans and pushed his cock toward Boone's waiting mouth. Gabe also got one good pull. Boone held out his oil-slicked hands and helped the two men into the tub. Thankfully, Rex had bought one of the biggest garden tubs they made. The three of them fit perfectly. Rex leaned against the back of the tub with Boone leaning back on his chest. Gabe leaned against the opposite side and put his feet between Boone's outstretched legs.

Rex reached for the washcloth he'd put on the side of the tub and began soaping it. He started at Boone's neck and face, being extra careful of the white gauze pad over his stitches and worked his way down to his shoulders. Rex spent a large amount of time just enjoying the play of muscles in Boone's shoulders and chest. He ran the cloth over every well-defined muscle. He moved slowly down his abdomen and right to his heavy cock. He ran into Gabe's feet.

Rex looked up at Gabe and grinned. "Are you trying to jack him off with your feet or just toe-fuck him?" While Rex waited for Gabe's answer he bit the tendon on the side of Boone's neck.

Gabe looked affronted. "Hey, you're the one that gets to do all the washing. I just figured I'd keep myself busy in the meantime." He slowly moved his toe up the crack of Boone's ass. "Am I bothering you, Boone?"

Boone's answer to the question was to move his legs to the outside of Rex's. "Nothing you do to my body will ever bother me, gorgeous."

Gabe gave Rex a "so there" look and continued exploring with his feet. "This is nice," Gabe said, looking around the tub. "Why haven't we done this before, baby?"

Rex lifted one side of his mouth in that sexy as sin grin he did so well. "Guess we've been too busy fucking, working or sleeping to do much relaxing. I guess we need to change that, don't we? Make the time to just cuddle up together and talk and stuff."

Gabe actually stuck his toe into Boone's hole. "Yeah, we need more time for the stuff part especially."

Boone thrust his ass into Gabe's foot and moaned. "Fuck, that feels good."

Gabe saw that Boone's eyes were half-lidded and didn't know whether it was lust or fatigue. He figured either one required a bed. "Rex, you'd better hurry up and get Boone washed. I think he's ready for bed."

Boone pushed into Gabe's foot again. "Yeah, take me to bed."

Rex soaped the cloth again. "Stand up so I can get the rest of you." Boone reluctantly removed Gabe's toe from his ass and stood. Rex quickly soaped the rest of him and then just to be a tease he stuck his finger all the way up Boone's ass.

"Fuck," Boone said and thrust his cock into the air. He looked back at Rex and got out of the tub. He pulled towels off the warmer and passed them out. They all quickly dried off and moved as one toward the big king-size bed.

Gabe positioned Boone in the center of the bed between him and Rex. They both started feeling Boone's skin. Their hands wandered around his entire body with a few pinches and licks thrown in. Gabe watched as Boone's cock began to harden. He looked over at Rex. "We need to talk before we fuck you, Boone. You both know that after we fuck we all just melt into a pile of goo and go to sleep."

Rex scooted closer to Boone as did Gabe. They both put their arms around him. Rex rested his head on his hand. He bent and kissed Boone then leaned over and kissed Gabe. At his nod Gabe began to fill Boone in on their plans for the future.

"Rex and I were talking about the future of the ranch. We've come up with a way to turn what Buck Baker made evil and ugly into something beautiful and special. We'd like to open an equestrian rehabilitation center here on the ranch. We'll still keep cattle for our day-to-day living expenses but we thought that we could use the revenue from the oil lease and outside sources to fund the center. We feel strongly that it should be a nonprofit center." Gabe looked down at Boone. Unable to read his expression he looked over at Rex for help.

Rex cleared his throat and continued with their plan. "We're going to redo this house for my mom and build another house for the three of us. We also discussed whether we should build some sort of temporary housing for the guests that we hope will come from farther away." He looked down at Boone. "I know it would probably mean changing your major again back to rehabilitation but you sounded like that was what you really wanted to do with your life." When they still got no response from Boone, Rex turned Boone's head so he could look him in the eye. "Talk to us, Boone. Do we have it all wrong? Is that it?"

Boone closed his eyes. His entire body tensed and shook with suppressed emotion. When he opened his eyes Gabe could see the raw emotion in them. He just couldn't quite read which emotion they were dealing with. "Boone?"

Boone licked his lips and ran a hand down his face. "I don't know what to say. Hell. I don't even know what to feel. I know you both told me that you wanted me here with you but why would you change your entire lives for me?"

Gabe leaned down and kissed him. "It's not just for you, Boone, and we won't be changing our entire lives. We'll still have the horses and cattle to take care of. We'll probably have to hire a few more people for the rehabilitation center or maybe we could even get some local folks to volunteer once in a while. You're part of this family now, Boone, and this ranch and your dreams were both meant for good. Hearing you talk about Tim and the joy he got out of riding a horse has inspired us to share that joy with others."

Boone lifted his arms behind both men's heads and brought them to him. He kissed Gabe and then Rex. "I think the plan is beautiful and I'll gladly work night and day to make the dream come true but it will take a lot of money to refurbish this ranch. I've got a lot of it but if the center is going to last for the long haul we'll have to find more."

Gabe smiled. "I've got a friend whose wealth surpasses even yours, and like you, he hasn't touched the money. I thought we could go talk to him and see if he'd be interested in investing in the center. My guess is that he's just been waiting for something worthwhile to spend his money on." Gabe ran his hand down Boone's chest to circle his cock. "Will you be able to switch majors without having to make up a lot of hours? Because we want you here with us, not in Tulsa at school."

Boone spread his legs over the top of Gabe's and Rex's. Rex was licking his nipples and Gabe was stroking his rigid cock. Damn, how had he gotten so lucky? He watched the muscles in Gabe's strong arms flex as he stroked him. "I'd need to make a trip to Tulsa to meet with my advisor but I chose geology in the first place because I already had taken the science and liberal arts requirements when I was in the rehabilitation program. I might even be able to take some classes online. If not I guess we can hire a specialist and I could just run the center because I don't want to be in Tulsa either."

Gabe liked Boone's answer so much he thought it deserved a blowjob. He kissed Boone's lips and went straight for his cock.

Chapter Eleven

ꕤ

Gabe called Jake the next morning to tell him about the house. Boone was in the kitchen working on his laptop and Rex was out taking care of the cattle. He was just about to give up when Jenny answered the phone.

"Hello."

"Hey, sweet Jenny, how're ya feeling?" Gabe took the phone over and stretched out on the couch.

"Gabe. I'm so glad you called. We need you to come to New Mexico for a wedding."

"I may be wrong but I distinctly remember attending your wedding, Jenny."

"Not mine, you goof. Ben's. He's getting married to Kate on Sunday. Come on, Gabe, you've got to be here."

Gabe smiled. "I never thought I'd see the day that old Ben would be gettin' married. But uh…Kate doesn't seem like his usual type of woman."

"Well, duh. Why do you think he's finally getting married? He found a jewel instead of his usual trash. So does that mean you'll come?"

"I wouldn't miss it for the world. How're they doing with Kate's problems with that Clint guy?" Gabe heard a whoop come from the kitchen and looked over. He could barely make out Boone at the table. He was excited about something he'd evidently found on the internet. Gabe's hand unconsciously went to the growing bulge in his jeans.

"Not good, I'm afraid. I'm sure the guys will want to talk to you about it when you get here. Do you want to talk to Jake? Cree's down at the station but Jake's just trying to sneak a cookie. He stupidly thinks just because I'm on the phone I must be blind."

Gabe continued to rub his cock through his jeans. "Put that rascal on the phone. Love ya, Jenny."

"Love you too, Gabe."

Gabe managed to get his jeans down and his naked cock in his hand before Jake got on the phone. He watched Boone concentrate on his computer as he stroked his cock. Those little reading glasses perched on Boone's nose were sexy as hell. He heard Jenny teasing Jake in the background.

"Hi, buddy. How's it hangin'?"

Gabe looked down at his cock. "Stiff as a board, old friend."

"Damn. That means either you're not getting any or you're getting a lot. So which is it?"

"I'm in love, Jake, and it's the real thing." He ran his thumb over the head of his dick. Jake and Cree were the only team members who knew he was gay.

"So who's the lucky guy?"

"Not guy. Guys. Rex Cotton and Boone Fowler. He's the geologist Rex and I brought in to check out an old oil well Buck started years ago."

"Damn, Gabe. Two guys? Fuck, that sounds hot. I never knew Cotton was gay. Cree and I used to enjoy watching him work, if you know what I mean."

"Yeah, I know exactly what you mean. That cowboy has one fine body. It's even better naked. Just wait 'til you meet Boone."

"So you're all three coming this weekend, right?"

"I'll have to check with them but I don't see a problem with it." Gabe took a deep breath. "Listen, Jake. The reason I called was to tell you that Buck's house burned down yesterday. It was an accidental blessing. I just hope there wasn't anything in the house that you wanted because the whole thing burned to the ground."

"Good riddance, I say. But where are you sleeping now?"

"I haven't slept in the main house for about three and a half weeks. We were pretty much just using it for storage. I'm sorry, Jake. I just couldn't sleep there. Too many things went on inside it." Gabe thought of the file on Jenny he'd found. No telling what else he would have eventually dug up in that house.

"I don't blame you for not sleeping there. I'll tell Jenny but don't worry. I'm sure she feels the same way I do. When do you think you'll make it to town?"

"We'll leave here after chores Saturday morning most likely. I'll ask Bob Henderson to check on the animals' food and water while we're gone."

"Sounds good, buddy. We'll see you then."

Gabe hung up the phone and walked to the kitchen with his jeans still pushed to mid-thigh. He came up behind Boone and nudged him in the side with his erection.

Boone stopped typing and looked down at his side. He looked up at Gabe and raised his brow. "Is that your way of asking me to help you with your problem?"

Gabe gave him a broad grin. "Just wondering if you were still busy. I just got off the phone with Jenny and Jake. Unless you have other plans I'd like you and Rex to come with me to Ben's wedding this weekend."

"I'd follow you anywhere. Now…about this problem…"

* * * * *

That evening at the supper table Gabe filled Rex in on his phone conversation with Jake. Rex rubbed his jaw. "Does Jake know about the three of us? Because I won't go if I have to hide it."

Gabe rubbed Rex's crotch with his bare foot under the table. "Sure, he knows. He's happy for us. Believe me when I say that is one family you'll never have to worry about as far as passing judgment. I think I've walked in on more blowjobs between the three of them than I'll get in a lifetime."

Rex chuckled. "I've walked in on a couple of those myself. Back when both of them were kids just learning what their dicks were for."

Gabe continued to rub Rex under the table but turned his head toward Boone. "So you never told me what got you so excited about this afternoon while you were on your laptop."

Boone smiled. He was perfectly aware of what was going on under the table. "Do you mean before or after you came in and shoved your cock down my throat?"

Rex looked from Boone to Gabe. "Dammit, Gabe. Tomorrow you're going out to do chores and I'm gettin' the afternoon blowjob."

Gabe and Boone laughed and threw their napkins at Rex.

Boone stood and started carrying dishes to the sink. "I found a couple of government programs that might help us with the center. I'll have to write up a proposal but there are grants available for making existing buildings handicapped accessible. I also looked up some building plans for the guest housing. I found these miniature log cabins that they use as motel cabins. They come in a kit with everything you need to build them. I thought the guests would rather have their own little cabin than to share one big building. It will seem more like a retreat to them instead of actual therapy. They have kits for bigger buildings as well. If we ordered one of those we could have one central place where they could all gather for downtime and meals."

Boone reached into the stack of papers on the counter and pulled out several sheets. "The plans that I printed show everything that's included in the kits. We might need to talk to the company about making the doorways larger and we can install the bathroom sink so it's wheelchair friendly along with the shower and toilet. I thought I'd get in touch with them tomorrow. Hell, they may even give us a break on the price. It could be good publicity for them." He pushed the papers over to Rex and Gabe.

Gabe and Rex looked over the plans. Boone even had a hand-drawn aerial view of the ranch yard and where he would locate the new buildings. Gabe looked over at Boone. "You've been quite the busy boy today. Can you try your best to put some figures to these new buildings before we leave Saturday? I'd like to give Ben a good idea of what we're doin' before I beg him for money."

"I could give him a lot more than just the figures for residential buildings if the two of you were willing to give up a few of your sex hours to help me with some more research. I'd like to have the rest of the estimates done as well. I'm talking about all the asphalt we'll need in the ranch yard and the new indoor arena. Not to mention trying to come up with someone to rework twenty or so saddles and getting enough horses for the patients. We might even ask around and try to find some people to donate old working horses. They could write it off on their taxes as a charitable donation."

Gabe and Rex grinned at each other. Gabe shook his head. "Boy, when you give Boone an idea he certainly doesn't let grass grow under him. What kind of research do you need help with?"

"Well, I'll need one of you to get in touch with an asphalt contractor and get him out here to give us a bid. The other one of you can call around to different construction companies. I'm thinking the new main house, horse barn and arena should be done by professionals. As well as the actual rehabilitation facility. We'll need all the normal exercise and therapy equipment if we're going to get any money from insurance companies or the government. The more money they are willing to pay the less it will cost us and our backers."

Boone shook his head. "I'm getting sidetracked again. Now. Back to the bids. I was hoping if we had them also build the majority of the guest housing that we could finish the inside stuff ourselves. We'd save a ton of money that way and maybe get some volunteers even to come in and help. There's always corporations looking for charity work as sort of a team building for their employees. Maybe one of you could start calling around."

Rex rose and leaned over the table to kiss Boone. "I'm exhausted just listening to you. Are you sure we're not biting off more than we can chew with this whole thing?"

"Trust me, Rex. It's going to be perfect."

* * * * *

Armed with estimates and tentative building plans, they set out for New Mexico four days later. They'd done very little sleeping and very little fucking in the past four days trying to get everything together. Rex smiled to himself. Who knew Boone could be such a slave driver?

They crossed into New Mexico and pulled in to a little roadside diner to get some lunch. Rex stretched his tired muscles as he got out of the truck. "I'm getting too old for this."

Gabe raised a brow. "What's that, old man? You mean you can't keep up with us young studs anymore?"

"Smart-ass. I'm just sayin' that all work and no play makes Rex a very grouchy boy."

Gabe blew him a kiss. "We'll make it up to you later tonight. Now stop bitchin' and let's eat."

Shortly before three o'clock they pulled in to the Triple Spur. "Wow…nice place." Boone's eyes were fixed on the impressive ranch house in front of them.

Gabe chuckled and squeezed his knee. "Now you see why I want Cree to design our new home." Rex stopped the truck and Gabe jumped out. He waited for Boone to get out and took his hand. "Come on, honey. Come meet some of my other family."

Gabe and Boone waited at the top of the stairs for Rex to join them. "Come on, baby." When Rex made it to the top of the steps, Gabe knocked on the front door. He squeezed both of his lovers' hands as he waited for someone to open the door. He was just about to give up and go check the barn when the door swung open. A very disheveled Cree stood in front of them.

"Hey, guys. We didn't expect you this early. You must've made good time. Come on in." Cree stepped back and let them enter.

Gabe took in his appearance and gave him a knowing look. "Where's Jake and Jenny?"

Cree started tucking his shirt in and smiled sheepishly. "Jenny's over at Kate's and Jake's in the study but he should be out any minute. Hi, Cotton." He shook Rex's hand and then turned toward Boone. "And you must be Boone. I've heard a lot of good things about ya." He ushered the men into the kitchen.

Gabe made himself right at home and dug five beers out of the fridge. "I'm glad to see that Jenny's allowing you to have beer in the house again."

Cree took one of the bottles as Gabe passed them out. He set Jake's down on the table. "Yeah, well, she decided she'd rather Jake and I drank in here as opposed to the barn. It seems she was on to our little stash out there. So tell me what you've been up to besides burning down that old bastard's house."

Boone tensed and looked toward Gabe. Gabe caught his eyes and reached out to squeeze his hand. "Don't worry, Boone. I told you they wouldn't be mad about the house."

"Mad? Hell no, I'm not mad. I just wish I could have been there to see it. Maybe done a little dance in the firelight. Don't worry, Boone. You're among friends here. We all love Gabe like a brother. You're a part of his family which makes you a part of ours. Same goes for you, Cotton."

Rex took a long pull off his beer. "Thanks, Cree. I wasn't sure if it would seem weird to you guys or not. My being with Gabe, I mean."

Cree laughed. "Not weird in the way you're thinkin', Cotton. Jake and I beat off many times to the sight of you without a shirt on. Why we used to—"

"Um…Cree, can we not go there please." Gabe interrupted Cree's trip down memory lane.

Cree realized what he started to reveal and blushed. "Sorry, Cotton."

Jake stepped into the kitchen just in time to save Cree any more embarrassment. "Hey, guys." He shook hands with Cotton and Gabe.

Gabe reached for Boone. "Jake, I'd like you to meet Boone Fowler. Boone, this scoundrel is Jake Sommers." He looked at Jake. "You are officially Jake Sommers now, aren't you?"

"Yep. As of last Tuesday. Nice to meet you, Boone." Jake pulled up a chair beside Cree. "Hey, is that beer for me?"

Cree nodded and handed him the beer. "So let me be the first to fill you guys in on the little fucker's latest."

At Boone's confused look Gabe leaned toward him and kissed his cheek. "The little fucker is their pet name for the asshole who's been harassing Kate."

At Boone's nod of understanding Cree went on to fill them in on the latest news. Halfway through the story Jake got up and passed out another beer to everyone. When Cree was finished everyone just sat back and took a long drink of their beer.

Finally Gabe broke the silence. He looked from Cotton to Boone. "All my friends fall in love with people who have other people out to either hurt them or kill them. I trust I'm not going to have to go through any of that crazy bullshit with either of you, am I?"

Rex leaned over and kissed him. "You're my first love so I don't think you have to worry about anyone in my past." Rex looked over at Boone. "What about you, Boone?"

Boone shyly kissed Gabe on the other cheek. "Ditto for me, Gabe. Although the foreman at the Flying Duchess wasn't too happy about me selling the place. I don't think he'd ever come after me."

Jake leaned on the kitchen table. "The Flying Duchess?"

Boone nodded. "My family's ranch in south Texas. I put it on the market a week ago."

"Oh fuck. You're talking about *The* Flying Duchess. Damn, man, that's one of the biggest ranches in the southwest. You own that?" Cree elbowed Jake in the side.

"Close your mouth, Jake, before you make a fool of yourself."

Boone smiled and gripped both Gabe's and Rex's thighs under the table. "I inherited the ranch when my father died but I haven't been there since I was seventeen and he threw me out of his house."

Jake nodded in understanding. "Yeah, I get where you're coming from. I had the same kind of relationship with my father."

Jake looked over at Cree to make sure he wasn't going to be elbowed again. "So do you mind me asking what you guys have planned for the future?" He nodded toward Gabe. "Gabe already assured me that you three definitely have a future together."

Boone smiled for the first time since he entered the house. He began telling Jake and Cree all about their dream of opening a riding facility for the handicapped. When he finished telling them about the facility Gabe took over.

"We're planning on talking to Ben about helping us fund the facility. We've worked hard all week and we came prepared with all the facts and figures to back up our proposal." Gabe leaned back in his chair and ran his hand down Boone's back.

Cree nodded and tipped his beer toward Boone, Gabe and Rex. "I'm sorry that we're not financially able to help you out with it. It sounds like a worthwhile undertaking." He looked over at Jake. "We will however be happy to supply some of the much-needed manpower that you're going to need before you can open."

Boone's eyes welled up with unshed tears. He cleared his throat. "Thank you both. I'm sure we'll need all the muscle we can get. It's a big project and the more we can do ourselves the better off the center will be financially." He looked from Gabe to Rex before continuing. "I feel it's only fair to tell you the story behind the facility." Boone went on to tell Cree and Jake about his brother and the need for the riding therapy. When he was finished he realized there wasn't a dry eye in the room.

Jenny picked that moment to enter the kitchen. "What the hell happened? I left two strong men in charge of the house and I come home to a kitchen full of crying sissies." She looked at the men's faces and went red. "Oh God, I'm sorry. Did something happen? I wasn't seriously making fun of you guys... I mean, I like that you guys are in touch with your feelings. Oh shit, I'll just shut up now."

Gabe rose from the table and grabbed Jenny up into a bear hug. "Hi, sweet Jenny. You're still the spitfire that we all remember." He motioned to Boone. "I'd like you to meet one of the loves of my life. This is Boone Fowler. Of course you remember my other love..."

"Cotton!" Jenny stepped out of Gabe's embrace to throw herself into Rex's outstretched arms. "I've missed you, Cotton."

"How've ya been, Miss Jenny?" Rex kissed her on the cheek.

Jake stepped in to take Jenny from Rex. "That's Mrs. Jenny now, Cotton. Now get your hands off my wife."

Rex shook his head. "Still the same ole Jake you always were. You never liked other people touching your stuff."

"Yeah, well, my *stuff* is still off-limits."

* * * * *

They ate grilled steaks and baked potatoes for dinner before sitting down to play cards. Gabe still refused to play poker with Jenny, claiming she was either the luckiest card player in the world or the sneakiest cheat he'd ever met.

At eleven o'clock the group decided to retire to their bedrooms for the evening. Cree showed Gabe, Boone and Rex to the bedroom at the end of the hall. Gabe was thankful they'd have some privacy.

Cree called goodnight to them and shut the door. They all undressed and headed for the shower. Gabe knew from staying at the Triple Spur in the past that Cree and Jake didn't do anything halfway. The bathroom was spacious with an extra-large walk-in shower.

Gabe turned on the faucet and turned to Rex and Boone. "C'mere, loves. I need to feel you tonight." Gabe kissed each of them while holding both bodies against his. When the shower was hot enough they all moved inside.

Rex grabbed the bottle of liquid soap and started running his hands up and down his lovers' bodies. While he was cleaning them, Gabe and Boone were busy kissing and nipping each other. Rex positioned the men under the spray to rinse them off. When all traces of soap were gone he quickly washed himself before kneeling in front of the two men.

Rex moved from one cock to the other, teasing both of them. When they'd had enough teasing they pulled Rex up into their embrace. "Love you two."

Gabe kissed Rex, sliding his tongue deep into Rex's mouth. "Love you, baby. Need you."

Rex smiled and reached over to the soap shelf. He held up a bottle of waterproof lube. "I think we owe our hosts a hearty round of applause." He poured some of the lube into both his hands and reached behind Boone and Gabe. Each hand went to work opening up one of his lovers.

Boone moaned and reached out to stroke Rex's cock. "Feels good, cowboy."

Gabe spread his legs a little more and thrust his cock against Rex's thigh. "Fuck me, baby."

Rex pulled his fingers out and positioned himself behind Gabe. He positioned Gabe behind Boone. "Boone, you'd better have a good hold on something because I feel like pounding the hell out of Gabe's ass. Which also means that Gabe will be pounding the hell out of yours."

Boone bent over and braced his hands out in front of him and his feet against the sides of the shower. "Ready."

Gabe lined his cock up with Boone's hole and slowly pushed his way past the tight ring of muscles inside his hot body. "Oh honey…feels good."

Rex positioned his cock and drove inside Gabe in one hard thrust. "Oh fuck." He withdrew his cock and slammed in again. After a few strokes the threesome established a steady hard, pounding rhythm.

Boone was the first to lose it, which set off a chain reaction. Gabe soon followed Boone and Rex a few strokes after that.

They collapsed onto the floor of the shower in a heap. Boone nuzzled Rex's neck. "I love you guys. Now I really need a bed. Give me a couple hours of shuteye and I'll be ready for more."

Chapter Twelve

The next morning they ate breakfast and headed over to Ben's. They all had a good laugh over the crates of chicken littering the farm. It seems Ben wanted to buy Kate new chickens to replace the one that had been poisoned and like everything Ben did the number of chickens he bought was way too large. Gabe agreed to take six chickens back with them.

Remy showed up about an hour before the ceremony was to begin. He pulled up in his rented SUV already wearing a suit. Gabe went over to welcome his fellow team member. "Hey. How're you doing, Remy?"

Remy flashed his killer smile. "Good to see you again, Gabe. Cree told me you be in looove just like our Ben. I remember Cotton right good but who dis new guy?"

Gabe smiled back and motioned for Boone to join them. "Remy Boudreaux, I'd like you to meet Boone Fowler."

"Woo weee! You're a hot one. Good thing I'm not stickin' around, I might have been tempted to change my spots." Remy looked at Gabe and winked. "I'm a lot prettier dan dis guy anyway."

Boone shuffled his feet in embarrassment. A steady growl emanated from Gabe's throat. "Yeah, it's a damn good thing you're not stayin', Cajun. You may be prettier than me but I'm a hell of lot tougher than you."

Boone pulled him back from Remy, unsure about the byplay between the two friends. Gabe looked over his shoulder at Boone and chuckled. "Relax, honey. We're just playin'. It's an old game. Although in the past it was always Remy afraid I was trying to take away his girlfriends."

"Liar."

* * * * *

After the wedding Gabe asked Ben for a couple minutes of his time. Ben gave Kate a kiss and excused himself. He ushered Gabe into his office. "So what's on your mind, Gabe?"

Gabe opened Boone's briefcase and pulled out the file. "I know it's not exactly the best day for this but I'd like you to listen to a business proposal. If I didn't think it was important I wouldn't even bring it up on your wedding day but I think it's a project that might appeal to you."

Gabe went on to tell Ben about Boone's brother and their plans to open the riding facility. He showed Ben the estimates they'd accumulated and the building plans. When he was finished Ben had a smile on his face. Gabe let out a breath.

Ben approached Gabe and settled a hand on his shoulder. "I think it would be beneficial to all concerned that I help as much as I can. The taxes are killing me and I'm sure my accountant would be thrilled at the deductions I could take. I also like the idea of my money going toward something so life-changing. The riding facility may not help people walk again but it could do worlds of good for their self-esteem." Ben shook Gabe's hand. "Count me in, buddy. I'll contact my lawyer early this week and get a special account established. You can draw from that account to get things started."

Ben walked toward the study door with Gabe by his side. He stopped Gabe with a hand on his forearm. "I'm happy for you, Gabe. It looks like your two men have been good for you."

"Thanks, Ben. I wish you and Kate all the happiness in the world."

* * * * *

After the reception everyone except Ben and Kate went back to the Triple Spur along with the keg of beer. The rowdy group of team members, along with their loved ones, sat on the porch and told stories of past adventures.

Mac, Nicco's business partner, had a few of his own about the years he was a Green Beret. Gabe noticed Nicco's face while Mac was talking. Gabe knew that look. It was the same look he had on his face every morning since falling in love.

They were just getting ready for bed when Gabe heard the phone ring in the hallway. He heard Remy's voice and then a shout that Ben's house was on fire.

The next several hours were spent fighting the fire at Ben's ranch and then searching for the man who set the fire. Gabe and Boone rode with Jake. Ben had asked Rex to take Kate back to the Triple Spur and watch her. When Cree finally radioed that he found the suspect at the hospital being treated for burns, the rest of the tired group went back to the Triple Spur. When they walked in the door they found Jenny and Kate in the kitchen cooking breakfast. Rex sat at the kitchen table drinking a cup of coffee.

Gabe walked over and gave him a kiss. "Morning, baby."

Rex kissed Gabe and then Boone. "Morning. Why don't the two of you go get cleaned up? Breakfast is about ready, so keep it short." He looked at Gabe and Boone as if reading their minds. "Showers only. You can take care of the other stuff later. I'm sure we'll all be ready for a long nap."

Gabe winked at him and kissed him again. "Sure thing, boss."

* * * * *

The threesome stayed at the Triple Spur until Tuesday afternoon. They wanted to show their support for Kate, Ben's new wife. She'd been having trouble with the town banker. He'd raped her when they were younger and it seemed he was up to his old tricks again. Clint Adams—or as Ben called him, "the little fucker"—was scheduled to appear in court that afternoon. Kate was trying to get a protection order against him and the three of them wanted to be in court for it. They headed back to Oklahoma the same evening.

Gabe looked over at the two men beside him. He still couldn't figure out how he'd gotten so damn lucky. For years he'd yearned for a family of his own. In the beginning, every foster home he was sent to gave him hope that maybe this family would keep him but after several years of hoping he gave up the thought of having a family of his own. Then he'd met Jenny. Seeing her with Cree and Jake made him yearn all over again.

He thanked God that he took the financial risk and bought the Double B. He knew his family was an unconventional one but it worked. Family should be made up of people who loved and respected one another and he'd found just that with Rex, Boone and Maggie.

He looked to his shoulder again. Boone was sound asleep. He'd been so excited that Ben believed in the facility enough to help fund it. It was clear to both him and Rex that Boone had never had any real friends. Gabe smiled and kissed the top of his blond head. He had a lot of friends now. Boone got a chance to see firsthand what friends would do for other friends.

Rex reached over Boone to put his hand on Gabe's thigh. "You okay, sweetheart?"

Gabe covered Rex's hand with his own. "I'm great, baby. Just thinkin' how lucky I am to have found the perfect family for myself. Thinkin' about how much I love you and Boone and of course our sweet Maggie."

Rex squeezed his thigh and let go. "We all love you too, Gabe. I plan on showing you just how much as soon as we get home." He winked and put his hand back on the steering wheel.

Rex turned the radio down. "So what part of the facility do you think we should tackle first?"

Gabe rubbed his jaw in thought. "Well…I'll call first thing in the morning to have the old house leveled and trucked away and then I say we start making our home wheelchair accessible. I'd like to start right away on the new house but Cree's going to need time to design it. With Ben's house burning down he's got two houses to design now. I'd rather be patient and wait on one of his designs than to settle for some other architect."

"I agree. For now let's widen the doorways and rework the bathroom at our house for Mom. We'll also need to put in a wheelchair ramp and maybe get started on some of the asphalt work. At least a path to the barn. I wouldn't do the rest until after building the other structures. Those big trucks can really tear up asphalt but I'd like Mom to at least be able to get to the barn."

"Sounds like a good plan, baby." Gabe rested his head on the back of the seat.

* * * * *

He must have dozed off because the next thing he knew Rex was shaking his thigh. "Wake up, lazybones."

Gabe opened his eyes to see they were already home. He looked over at Rex and Boone. Boone looked like he'd just been woken too. Gabe looked down at the drool stain on his t-shirt and chuckled. "Damn, Boone. I'm going to start making you wear a bib."

Boone elbowed him in the ribs. "I thought you liked my spit."

"I do. In my mouth…on my cock…in my ass. Just not running down my shoulder." He opened the truck door. "Let's get inside and see if we can find something constructive for all that excess spit to do."

They got their duffels out of the truck bed and stumbled to the house in a sleepy fog. Throwing their bags on the floor of the bedroom, they quickly undressed and snuggled under the covers. Gabe could tell that Rex was beyond tired so he decided to take care of him first. He wrapped his fingers around Rex's semi-hard cock as he ran his tongue over the seam of his lips.

Rex immediately went hard and opened his mouth. Gabe thrust his tongue into the warm depths and groaned. "Mmm…you taste good, baby."

Gabe felt Boone's hands brush over his to cradle Rex's heavy sac. Rex groaned and thrust his pelvis into both of their hands. "Love you two."

Boone joined the kiss. Three tongues lapping and probing made for a very sloppy kiss. Gabe broke off from the kiss to lean over and take Rex's nipple between his teeth. He bit down with just enough pressure to sting.

"Uhhh…gonna come." Rex panted and thrust his hips as fast as he could.

Boone slipped behind Rex's sac to his puckered opening. He eased two fingers in at the same time and Rex's balls drew up.

Gabe saw that Rex was about to come and replaced his hands with his mouth. He swallowed as much of Rex's cock down his throat as he could and hummed. He smiled to himself as Rex pumped his essence down his throat. The humming thing got Rex every time.

Rex was so tired that he fell asleep as soon as he came. Boone looked over at Gabe and climbed over Rex to cuddle against him. He took Gabe's mouth in a tender kiss. "Thank you for talking to Ben about the facility. No one's ever gone to bat for me like that before."

Gabe ran his finger across the healing wound on Boone's forehead. "No need to thank me, honey. We're family now. Rex and I decided our first priority was to modify the house so we can bring Maggie home."

Boone nodded. "We should get started first thing in the morning. I like Maggie and I like the way you are when you're around her."

"What am I like?" Gabe brushed Boone's long hair over his shoulder. He reached down to Boone's heavy erection and stroked him slowly.

"I dunno. Like a mischievous boy. Like you'd do anything to make her happy." He ground his cock against Gabe's hand. He spread his thighs and pulled Gabe between them.

Gabe kissed down Boone's neck and bit his shoulder. "I've never really had a mom. I guess that's why I have so much fun with Maggie. But enough about Maggie right now and pass me the lube. I want inside this fine ass of yours."

Chapter Thirteen

Four months later

ꙮ

Rex settled Maggie into bed for her afternoon nap and went in search of his men. He loved having his mom at the ranch but it put a bit of a cramp in their lovemaking. Their own house wouldn't be finished for about another three months.

At least the cabins were coming along nicely. The rest of the team was due to arrive tomorrow and the day after to help with the finishing touches on the guest cabins. Remy was even bringing Corrine with him this time. With a hurricane warning out for Key West they both decided to board up the bar and leave the island.

Rex couldn't wait to tell Gabe that she was coming. Gabe was just talking to Remy a couple weeks ago and it sounded like things between the two partners was starting to finally heat up.

He decided to look for Gabe in the barn first since the ranch truck was still parked out front. Before Rex even stepped foot inside the barn he knew both Gabe and Boone were inside. He heard Boone's pleas and Gabe's grunts fifty yards away. He quickened his step and looked around him. The construction workers were all busy with either the house or the rehabilitation building. The new horse barn and riding arena were finally completed. They'd brought in two construction companies. One company for their house and another for the rest of the work.

Rex unsnapped his favorite sleeveless chambray shirt as he entered the old barn. Dust motes hung in the air as if suspended by tiny threads from the rafters. He spotted the two rutting males in the back corner of the barn. Nowadays they all took release where and when they could get it. Usually either in the barn or in one of the cabins.

Pulling off his boots and jeans, Rex made his way to the back corner. Damn, he loved watching Gabe pound Boone's ass. He stood to the right of them unnoticed for a couple more minutes stroking his own cock. Boone's ass on display perfectly. Gabe's long, thick cock sinking in again and again. Poor Boone was getting a serious pounding today but apparently he was eating it up because he kept demanding more.

"Fuck, that's good, gorgeous. Harder." Unbelievably Gabe began to fuck him even harder. "Oh God…gonna come."

Rex wasted no time kneeling in front of Boone and swallowing his cock.

Boone looked down at Rex and smiled. "Love you. Suck me in deep because I'm about to come." With those words barely out of his mouth, Boone came down Rex's throat.

Gabe heard Rex's slurping sounds and came deep inside Boone. "Oh fuck…so good, honey." Gabe slid out of Boone and onto the floor, his hair soaked with sweat from the exertion.

Boone's cock slid from Rex's mouth as he knelt to kiss him. "Thank you, cowboy." He turned and kissed Gabe. "Good one, G." Boone pulled both men into his arms. "Love you guys."

Gabe wiped the sweat off his brow with his discarded shirt. "If we keep fuckin' in the barn I'm going to install an air conditioner. I think that last fuck cost me at least three pounds."

Rex grabbed Gabe's shirt and wiped his hand. Watching his lovers had excited him so much he spent himself like a schoolboy.

Gabe took his shirt back and swatted at Rex. "Come on, baby. I was going to wear that shirt. I can't go back in the house with cum stains all over myself. What would Maggie think?"

Rex laughed and looked for his jeans. "She's the one who told me to come find you guys. I think she knows what we've been doing in the barn twice a day." Rex slipped into his jeans and boots. Running his hand down his torso, he tweaked his own nipple and watched Gabe's eyes narrow.

"I came out to tell you that Remy called. He's bringing Corrine with him tomorrow. It seems there's a hurricane warning out for Key West so they decided to just board up the bar and both come up to help." He put his shirt on but left the snaps undone.

Gabe put his jeans on and helped Boone up. "I've gotta get into town and go to the grocery store before everyone gets here." He looked at Boone and Rex. "If either of you has errands to run you can ride with me."

Boone shook his head. "Can't, Gabe. I'm meeting the contractor who's putting in the new well in an hour. Do you mind picking up the paperwork for the oil lease from the lawyer's office while you're in town though?"

"Not at all, honey. What about you, baby?" Gabe ran his hand down Rex's back and squeezed his ass.

Rex shook his head and adjusted his cock. "Beds are being delivered anytime. I'm gonna have the delivery guys just put them in the various cabins and we can have our guests put them together when they get here tomorrow."

Gabe nodded and pulled Rex into an embrace. "I thought we'd give Ben and Kate the cabin with the queen-size bed and the rest of the guys can take the ones with the full-size beds." He gave Rex and quick kiss. "Did Remy say whether he would need one cabin or two?"

Rex squeezed Gabe's ass and pulled Boone into the hug. "He didn't say but then I can't understand half of what that guy says. I guess we ready two cabins and then give them the choice."

"I just wish my Jenny could come but Jake said she was too close to term to do much traveling. Cree's staying at the Triple Spur with her. Don't ask me how we're going to handle Jake for a week with no sex." Gabe swatted Rex's ass. "I've heard him talk about how hot he and Cree thought you were when they were younger. You just make sure he keeps his hands to himself. I'd dearly hate to have to kill one of my best friends."

Boone laughed but Rex could tell by the look in Gabe's eyes that he wasn't joking. He loved it that Gabe was so possessive. Rex ran his hands through Gabe's hair. "Hell, sweetheart...I can barely keep up with you two. I don't think it's very likely that I'd have enough energy left over to fool around with Jake. Besides, you know how much I love you."

Narrowing his eyes for a minute longer, Gabe kissed him and then Boone. "Mine...both of you."

* * * * *

Ben, Kate and Jake arrived the next afternoon. Gabe and Rex showed them to their cabins. Gabe opened the door to the biggest of the ten available cabins. "Still a little rustic but that's why we begged for your help." Gabe sheepishly looked at Kate. "We need a woman's opinion on decorating. We have the basics but we were kinda hoping you'd go online and into Styler for us and buy some decorating stuff for the cabins. We want to make rehabilitation guests feel comfortable."

Kate stood on tiptoes and kissed Gabe's cheek. When Gabe heard the slight growl from Ben he smiled. "I'd love to help you guys with that. I think the whole idea of this place is wonderful. Besides, I've shopped online for years. I know all the best places to go."

Ben put his arm around his new wife. He rubbed her tummy and kissed her. "Good. I'd rather have you and our baby in front of the computer than up on a roof."

Gabe, Rex and Jake all looked at the happy couple. Jake reached out and slapped Ben on the shoulder. "You old dog. I can't believe you didn't tell me you two were expecting."

Ben shrugged and nodded. "We just found out a couple weeks ago. I kinda wanted to tell you all together but I just couldn't hold it in any longer."

Rex and Gabe shook Ben's hand and kissed Kate on the cheek. "Congratulations to you both." Gabe looked at Kate and smiled.

Rex tipped his cowboy hat. "We'll just leave you two alone to unpack and get your bed set up."

The threesome walked to the next cabin. Rex opened the door for Jake and Gabe. "This'll be yours, Jake." Rex motioned to the small two-room cabin.

Gabe wrapped his arm around Rex and looked at Jake. "So you haven't told me yet how my sweet Jenny is?"

The look of love that crossed Jake's face made Gabe smile. "Gettin' real big. She's still got another month or so but twins are a little trickier. The doc says she needs to take it easy so she doesn't go into premature labor." Jake shrugged his shoulders. "We're also on a strict no-sex diet. It sucks. You guys are lucky you won't have to worry about it." Jake smiled and jabbed Gabe in the ribs with his elbow.

Rubbing his ribs, Gabe punched him in the arm. "Well, instead of a pregnant woman in the house we have Rex's mom, Maggie. She approves of us and everything but we tend to get a wee bit vocal so we've been keeping it mostly out of the house." Gabe looked at Rex and winked. "Does tend to get a little creative that way though."

Jake groaned and shook his head. "Yeah, I know what you mean. Cree and I've done it almost everywhere on the ranch. As long as it's away from the house."

Gabe happened to notice Jake's growing erection through his jeans. He cleared his throat and turned toward Rex. "We'll just let you settle in and get your bed put together. You might want to call Cree and take care of that problem of yours before dinner. Maggie's a sweet little thing. No sense shocking her."

* * * * *

As he sat at the dinner table surrounded by Gabe's friends, Boone couldn't help but feel a bit emotional. He'd met these people all within the last four months and they felt more like family to him than any real family could. He took a drink of his water and cleared his throat. "I'd like to thank you all for coming to help us out. The rehab center couldn't have been built without all of you."

Boone felt his eyes start to burn. He tried to clear the lump in his throat and continued. "Tim would have loved this place..." Tears started to slide down his cheeks and his embarrassment drove him from the table. "Excuse me."

Boone left the room and Gabe looked at Rex. He started to get up and Maggie motioned him back down. "Let me do it, son."

Maggie wheeled herself into the bedroom. She found Boone sitting on the edge of the bed blowing his nose. She put her frail hand on his knee. "No one here cares if you cry, Boone. Those that don't already love you soon will. And there's no need to hide emotions from those that love you."

Boone looked at Maggie. "Sometimes it's too much for me to take in. I went my whole life without this much love. Tim was the only one and when he died I shut myself off from any real emotion."

Maggie patted his knee and took his hand. "Tim would be proud of you. You've done a great thing here." When Boone started to protest Maggie shook her head. "Yes, you've had a lot of help but it's you who's responsible. Rex and Gabe love you more than anything in the world."

Maggie chuckled and shook her head. "I agree that it's an unconventional relationship but truer love I've never seen. And it's because of that love they want to help you with this center. Your brother was very important to you therefore he's important to them." She patted his hand once more. "Now get back on out there and enjoy yourself. Family doesn't hide their emotions."

Boone kissed Maggie's cheek. "I love you, Maggie. I'm glad you're here."

Laughing, Maggie looked back at him. "Even though I've put quite the crimp in your lifestyle?"

Boone's face flushed. "Even though."

"Well, I've been thinking that maybe I'd like to move out to one of the cabins as soon as you get them ready. Your house won't be finished for a while yet and I'd like you all to have a bit more privacy. The cabins are set up for wheelchairs so I shouldn't have any problems as long as I have a phone."

Boone pushed Maggie back into the kitchen. "Give us a couple days, Mags."

When they entered the kitchen both Rex and Gabe rose and embraced Boone. Kissing his eyes, Gabe sighed. "We love you, honey. We're all one big happy family now."

Rex nodded and kissed them both. Jake decided to ease the tension in the room. "Hey, guys, that's enough mushy stuff. Some of us have to sleep alone tonight."

Gabe pulled back just enough to look at Jake. "Damn right you do. These two are mine."

Ben piped up in his usual deep voice. "I don't share either, bro, sorry."

Jake smiled and winked at Maggie. Tickled pink at his actions, Maggie swatted him on the arm. "The spirit may be willing but the body knows you're too much for even me."

Rex turned red as his jaw dropped. "Gross, Mom."

Jake kissed Maggie's cheek. "Thanks, Maggie, but I've got a couple loved ones at home that wouldn't much like it either."

* * * * *

Around eleven o'clock the next morning, the rest of the gang showed up. Remy and Corrine drove in from the airport with Nicco and Mac. As the foursome piled out of the big black SUV, Gabe put down his hammer to go and greet them.

"Hey, guys, glad you could make it." He hugged Nicco and Mac. He looked at Remy for an introduction.

Remy put his arm around Corrine. "Gabe, I'd like you to meet Cory Badeau."

Gabe shook the pretty dark-haired woman's hand. "Pleasure to finally meet you, Cory." Gabe winked and motioned to Remy. "This guy's talked about you for years. It's nice to finally put a face with the name."

Remy pulled Cory closer to his side as the rest of the team joined them on the front porch of Rex's house. "So what do we do now? Looks good ta me." Remy looked out over the busy construction of the main house and rehab center.

Rex pointed toward the cabins. "We need help with the cabins mostly. Kate's going to help us with the actual decorating." He looked at Cory. "I'm sure she'd welcome the help if you're interested."

Cory smiled and bit her lip. "Thank you. I'd love to help in whatever way I can."

Rex smiled at her soft Southern accent. He could tell that she was raised in wealth. He wondered how she'd become friends with Remy. He shook his head and looked at Remy. "The cabins are up but they still need the insides finished. Stuff like the sinks and toilets put in. We've already put them in five of the cabins but the other five still need to be finished. There's also two cabins left that we agreed to put roof shingles on."

Remy nodded and scratched at his five o'clock shadow. "Guess it good tang I'm used to working on de toilets at de bar."

Gabe wrapped his arms around Rex from behind. He rested his head on Rex's shoulder. "Let's grab some lunch, then we can get started."

* * * * *

After lunch, the men set off to the various cabins to start work and Kate sat with Cory and Maggie at the kitchen table. Kate pulled up a few of the shopping sites she frequented on the internet. She glanced over at Maggie, a little curious. "So tell me, Maggie, how do you like living on the ranch so far?"

Maggie smiled. "I love it. I'd never tell Rex this but I hated that dreadful nursing home. The people were nice enough but I've always preferred to live in open spaces not in a building in the center of town. I enjoy looking out the window and seeing the open fields."

Kate nodded and pointed out some curtains she'd found. "What about...um..."

As if reading her mind, Maggie blushed and patted her hand. "I've never seen my son happier. When Gabe and Boone came into my Rex's world he began living for the first time in his life. I know others will look down on their relationship but they're all three fine men. Whose business is it who they love and what they do in their bedroom?"

Cory smiled at the two women. "My only objection to the threesome is they're all so hot I feel sorry for the women around here." She laughed and poured herself another glass of lemonade.

Kate looked over her laptop at Cory. "Remy's not half bad himself. It seems like you've managed to tame the 'Crazy Cajun'."

Cory waved her comment away with a brush of her hand through the air. "We've known each other all our lives. He was best friends with my husband growing up and I just sort of fell in with the two of them in elementary school. My husband Anton died over two years ago." Cory pushed a black curl behind her ear. "It wasn't until this past week that I felt ready to let Remy in. Even though we've loved each other for years I was afraid to give myself to another man."

Kate could tell the story went much deeper but she didn't want to pry. "Well, all I can say is you've also got one hot-lookin' man on your hands."

"Thank you, *cherie*," Remy's deep voice came from the doorway.

All three women looked toward the voice. Kate's face blushed a crimson shade. "Don't tell Ben I said that. He gets kinda territorial around other men."

Remy laughed and sat down beside Cory. He wrapped his arm around the back of her chair and leaned in for a good long kiss. Without saying another word, Remy stood and walked out the kitchen door.

Now it was Cory's turn to blush. She shrugged her shoulders at the women and went back to her laptop.

Chapter Fourteen

ꚛ

Three days later, Boone woke to find warmth surrounding his cock. He reached down and ran his fingers through Rex's short black hair. He thrust his cock deeper into the wet warmth of Rex's throat. "Damn. That feels fantastic, cowboy."

They'd moved Maggie into her own little cabin the day before and this moment made all the hard work worth it to Boone. He looked down past Rex's head to find Gabe rimming Rex's ass with his tongue. Boone reached for Gabe and tapped him on the shoulder. "Slide your sweet cock up my way, G. My mouth's feeling a little lonely."

Without taking his tongue out of Rex's hole, Gabe maneuvered his body so Boone could bend toward him on the bed and swallow his cock.

The room was filled with moans and slurping sounds. When Rex introduced his finger to Boone's hole, Boone thought he'd lose it right then. He pulled off Gabe's cock. "Fuck me, cowboy." He nibbled the tip of Gabe's cock. "I want in you, G."

Rex pulled off Boone's cock with a pop. He leaned over and withdrew the bottle of lube from the drawer and waited for Boone and Gabe to get into position. With Gabe on his back and Boone between his spread thighs, Rex squirted some lube onto his hand and ran his fingers around and in Gabe's hole. He finished the pair off with a quick lube to Boone's throbbing cock.

Next, he poured more lube into his hand and introduced two fingers to Boone's tight hole. Boone thrust back, taking his fingers even deeper. "Now," Boone cried as he entered Gabe's tight hole.

Rex waited for Boone to fully enter Gabe, then lined his own cock up with Boone's hole and pushed slowly inside. Boone's body seemed to pull Rex's cock in by itself. When he was buried to the root he slid out and held on to Boone's hips. He helped Boone into a nice slow rhythm that gave pleasure to all three men. Gabe's legs were thrown over Boone's shoulders and Rex had to be careful he didn't get a toe in the eye. The rhythm began to pick up speed and soon the sound of slapping balls filled the room. Gabe reached down and stroked his own cock to the quick pace set by Rex.

Boone's back was covered with sweat as he thrust back and forth. "Oh God…gonna come."

Rex plowed into him even harder. "Come for me, sweetheart. Milk my cock with your ass."

Like always, the dirty talk got Gabe off first and he blasted his cum up between himself and Boone.

With a roar to rival a lion Boone came next. The constriction around Rex's cock was too much and he shot deep inside Boone.

They collapsed to either side of Gabe. Finally, with their breathing under control, Rex leaned over and pulled his two lovers in for a three-way kiss. "Mmm…heaven on earth."

* * * * *

After they'd showered and changed they made their way into the kitchen. Kate and Cory were at the stove cooking breakfast. Ben and Remy were seated at the table drinking their morning cup of coffee along with Mac and Nicco.

Gabe went to the cupboard and took down three mugs. He poured coffee and set the mugs on the table in front of his loves. Taking a seat, Gabe looked around for Maggie and Jake. "Where's Maggie and Jake?"

Kate turned around with a spatula in her hand. "Maggie said she was just going to have some toast and tea this morning in her new room. She said she'd be out and about a little later."

Ben smiled and slapped Gabe on the back. "I believe Jake is making his usual morning phone call to Cree for release. I've never met a hornier man in my life. You'd think the guy couldn't go twenty-four hours without coming."

At that comment both Cory and Kate turned around and looked at Ben. All the men around the table began squirming in their chairs. Kate put her hand on her hip and addressed Ben. "Hello, pot? You're making a couple of kettles around the table uncomfortable."

Cory started laughing and went to give Remy a quick kiss. When he pulled her into his lap she squealed. "Remington Boudreaux, let me go."

"Never, *cherie*. Gonna hang on te you forever." He took her mouth in a deep kiss. Breaking the kiss, he looked around the table. "Sorry, fellas, but Remy doesn't share."

Cory pinched his nipple and rose from his lap. Jake came in as Remy was rubbing his sore nipple through his tight black t-shirt. Jake looked at Remy rubbing his nipple and turned on his heels and went back out the door.

The group watched him go, laughing. Nicco slapped the table and wiped a tear from the corner of his eye. "Shit, now he'll have to make yet another call to Cree and it'll be thirty minutes before he comes back."

Ben looked up at the women. "Quick. Get breakfast on the table. If he's not back before we eat I'm eatin' his share."

That sent another round of laughter around the room. Even Boone was loosening up around Gabe's former team members. He actually reached over and patted Ben's rock-hard stomach. "I don't imagine you'll need Jake's portion. I happen to know that Kate fixed you three portions of food already."

Ben smiled and swatted Boone's hand away. "Well, if she didn't make me burn so many calories trying to keep her satisfied I wouldn't have to eat so damn much." He reached out and swatted Kate's ass. "Ain't that right, baby?"

Kate lifted one eyebrow at Ben. "Keep it up and I'll put you on a diet…in more ways than one."

* * * * *

By the end of the week Ben, Kate and Jake had to say their goodbyes. Jenny was getting too close to giving birth for Jake to stay any longer. Besides the fact that he spent most of his time on the phone with Cree anyway.

All ten cabins were finished and the remaining group started on the large dining hall. The hall only consisted of four rooms. A large living room, dining room and industrial-size kitchen along with a restroom. Mac and Nicco decided to tackle the appliances in the kitchen while Cory put the finishing touches on the dining room.

Rex was off with the oil company representative and Boone was supervising the finishing touches to the third and final water well.

Gabe worked by himself in the living room. He was hooking up the big-screen television Mac and Nicco had donated to the satellite system they'd also donated. Gabe thought about his friends and shook his head. Who knew a guy like himself would find so much love in his life? Growing up he'd yearned for an eighth of the love he felt today. He remembered what Jake told him when he'd helped on the Triple Spur. Jake said, "Open yourself up to all possibilities and you'll find love."

Gabe smiled to himself. He thanked God every day that he'd opened himself to first Rex and then Boone. He couldn't imagine his life without them. Funny how being open to possibilities can change your life, he thought.

He finished up with the entertainment center and strolled through to the dining room. "Hey, Cory, it's looking great in here." He looked around at the large open-beamed dining room. Cory and Kate had done an outstanding job of finding big sturdy farmhouse-style oak dining tables. There were three in the room but only enough chairs for two of them. Most of their guests would unfortunately have their own but they'd decided to buy twenty chairs and scatter them around the three tables.

Cory put the last dried floral arrangement on the sideboard and turned toward Gabe. "Thank you, Gabe. I'm about done in here then I'll start on the living room. Have you seen Remy?"

Gabe nodded and headed for the kitchen. "He's in the bathroom fighting with the toilets." He winked at Cory over his shoulder. "I think the toilets are winnin'."

He pushed the kitchen door open and stopped in his tracks. Mac and Nicco were in a clinch in front of the big industrial refrigerator. Gabe couldn't tell whether or not they'd been kissing but they both had strange looks on their faces. He decided to back away quietly before they noticed him. He didn't know about Mac but he knew for sure that Nicco didn't think anyone knew he was gay. He'd wondered about the two of them for years and now he believed he had his answer.

Gabe strolled back through the living room. He waved at Cory. "I'm gonna go check on the house and then ride out to check on my men. I'll see you all at supper."

* * * * *

Gabe thought about riding Lolly out to find Rex and Gabe but settled on the pickup. His men were in two different corners of the ranch and it would take too long by horse.

He pulled his truck up to the new oil wells going up first. The oil company they'd sold the mineral rights to had been very accommodating. Once they'd told them they would be happy to knock off some of the lease price if they'd make their own road to the oil field the company agreed. It seems there might be quite a bit of oil under the Double B. The oil company wanted the oil but they didn't want the bad publicity of driving their semis through a ranch full of handicapped children.

All in all, it had worked out the best for both parties involved. Gabe spotted Rex talking to the foreman on the job site. The foreman was a pretty good-looking guy with close-cropped red hair. Gabe didn't much care for the way Rex was laughing at whatever the foreman was saying. A little of the green-eyed monster crept into his head and he stalked toward the pair.

He walked right up to Rex and before Rex could even acknowledge him Gabe grabbed the back of his neck and pulled him into a passionate kiss. "Mine," he growled in Rex's ear.

Rex rolled his eyes and kissed Gabe's nose. "Yours." Rex gestured to the redheaded man. "Gabe, I'd like you to meet Brian. He's the foreman for the oil company. Brian, this is one of my partners, Gabe."

Gabe reluctantly shook Brian's hand. "How much longer before the wells are completed?"

Brian wiped his forehead on his sleeve. "We've still got another three weeks on the batch we're currently drilling. If they prove as productive as we think we'll probably add a few more in the near future."

Gabe nodded and looked over at Rex. "You about done here?"

Rex smiled and nodded. "Sure, sweetheart." He shook Brian's hand and said his goodbyes.

Once they were on their way to the water wells Rex smiled and poked Gabe in the ribs. Gabe knocked his hand away. Rex went for the bulge in Gabe's jeans next. As he rubbed his hand across the soft denim he sighed. "I told you before you didn't have to worry about me being faithful, sweetheart."

Gabe didn't look at Rex but he spread his legs a little wider. "I didn't care for the way *Brian* was lookin' at you."

Rex smiled to himself and unbuttoned Gabe's jeans. He spread Gabe's jeans open and fished Gabe's poor neglected cock out. He sucked the tip into his mouth just as Gabe hit a rut in the old ranch road. Gabe's cock hit the back of Rex's throat.

Rex pulled off Gabe's cock and looked up at him. "Do you think it would be too much to ask for you to stop this damn truck until I'm finished? I'm rather fond of my tonsils, thank you very much."

Gabe stopped the truck and turned off the ignition. He turned sideways on the bench seat and, after shucking his boots, he slid his jeans down and off. Gabe put one leg on the dashboard and one leg over the back of the seat, presenting himself nicely for Rex. "How's this, baby? See anything you like?"

Rex growled and swallowed Gabe's cock once again. As he slid his mouth up and down on Gabe's shaft he clumsily took off his own boots and jeans. When he was naked from the waist down he pulled off Gabe's cock and kissed him. "Gonna fuck ya, sweetheart."

At Gabe's groan and nod, Rex spit into his hand and began preparing Gabe's tight hole. Gabe used his superior strength to lift his ass off the seat by using his legs and arms. Rex's mouth watered at the sight in front of him. Gabe's muscles glistened with sweat and stood out in golden mounds of strength. Each muscle clearly defined and undeniably his.

Rex got Gabe prepared and spit into his hand once more. Coating his own erection with his slick spit, he positioned himself and pushed inside Gabe. "You feel so good, sweetheart." He pumped into Gabe in long, hard strokes. "Love the way your ass squeezes my dick."

Gabe threw his head back and slammed it into the driver's window. "Fuck, baby. Ride me hard."

Rex put his hands under Gabe's lower back and helped hold him up as he pounded into his lover. Rex looked down and watched his dark brown cock disappear inside Gabe. Damn, that looked good. He glanced up at Gabe's weeping cock. "Better wrap your hand around that thing because I'm about to come."

Gabe did as instructed and fisted his own erection. After only a couple strokes he started to pant. "Can't hold it, baby. Gonna come all over us."

Rex pistoned his hips faster. He felt the hairs on the back of his neck begin to tingle as his balls drew up tight. "Now, sweetheart. Give it to me now."

Gabe exploded pearly white streams onto his chest as Rex groaned and buried himself as deep as he could inside Gabe. He marked his release with a roar of triumph. They both collapsed onto the truck seat as Rex continued to pulse stream after stream inside Gabe.

Gabe stroked Rex's cheek. "I love you. Can't help but to be jealous, you know."

Rex pulled out and ran his tongue up the side of Gabe's neck. He nibbled his way across Gabe's strong jaw to land on his lips. He thrust his tongue into Gabe's open mouth, kissing him with everything he had. "I love you too, sweetheart. And I'm sure I'd have been just as jealous if the tables had been turned."

Rex sat up and dug in the glove box for napkins. He cleaned them both up and they were dressed and on the road within five minutes.

* * * * *

They pulled up to site of the newest water well. Gabe smiled and looked over at Rex. "I can't believe our Boone found enough water for three wells. We'll have enough water in both the south and east pastures to satisfy two hundred and fifty head in each pasture year-round."

Rex nodded and looked out the windshield. Gabe could tell something was on his mind. "Talk to me, baby. What's wrong?"

Rex took off his cowboy had and ran his fingers through his silver and black hair. "Just wondering whether we need that many head. Five hundred is a lot of cattle to look after with just the two of us working the ranch. Especially since they'll be in two different pastures." He looked over at Gabe. "I'd like to enjoy my family a bit and I don't want to hire a new young stud cowboy to come in and help."

Gabe hadn't thought about it before but Rex was right. With the money from the oil wells coming in they didn't really need that many head to still make a nice living for themselves. "You're right, baby. I'd much rather spend the extra time with you and Boone. How many do you think we need to make a decent living for ourselves?"

Rex leaned over and kissed him. "Life would still be good with only about a hundred and fifty head per pasture. It would most likely give us a couple extra hours a day to spend with each other."

Gabe pulled Rex into his arms for a long, deep kiss. A bang to his driver's window had him turned with fists clenched in a split second.

Rex put his hand on Gabe's thigh. "Take it easy, sweetheart. It was just Boone throwing an empty pop can at the window trying to get our attention. It seems he's in need of rescuing."

Gabe exhaled audibly and looked toward Boone. He'd been cornered by Ashley Harrison, the daughter of the building supply company they used. Evidently old man Harrison had sent her out with the last of the supplies needed for the newest well. Gabe looked over at Rex.

"We've got two choices. We can get out of the truck and spoil her plans or we can come out to one of the biggest gossips in town. Of course if we just run her off she'll corner him again sooner or later."

Rex looked at poor Boone. Ashley had one hand on his chest and one hand running up and down his heavily muscled biceps. "How 'bout if only one of us comes out? I've known her all of her life and she's never put the moves on me." He winked at Gabe. "Your meat's just as fresh as Boone's so if I come out she'll just set her sights on you. I think you should do it…unless you don't want the town knowin'?"

Gabe squeezed Rex's thigh. "I'm not ashamed of who I love, baby." He opened the truck door. "I'll go save our man. After all I've been trained for the dangerous mission I'm about to embark on."

Gabe walked up to the pair and crossed his arms. "Something you need to tell me, honey?"

Boone let out a sigh of relief. "Hi, Gabe. Come over and give me some sugar." He shrugged Ashley's hands off his body and reached for Gabe.

Gabe went into his arms and Boone's mouth immediately covered his. They played tonsil hockey for Ashley's viewing pleasure. When Gabe stepped even closer and rubbed his now-hard cock against the front of Boone's faded jeans, Ashley gasped and stepped back.

"I'm sorry, Mr. Whitlock. I-I didn't know that you and, um…Mr. Fowler were um…a c-couple." She backed toward her truck with her eyes big as saucers. "Just send the check into the store or stop by sometime and pay my dad." Ashley jumped into the big flatbed delivery truck and sped off through the field.

Boone took Gabe's mouth again. "Thank you for saving me, G. That little minx wouldn't take no for an answer and I didn't want to out either you or Rex without your permission."

Gabe pulled Boone's button open and slid his zipper down. He knelt in front of Boone and pulled his rock-hard cock out of his jeans. He ran his tongue up the length of Boone's now-dripping cock.

Boone put his hands back against the stock tank that sat at the base of the new windmill. "Good, G. So damn good." He looked toward the truck just in time to see Rex sauntering over, stroking his own cock.

Rex stepped up to Boone and leaned in for a kiss. He faced his cock so it hit Gabe in the cheek and Gabe pulled off Boone's cock and began sucking Rex's. While he deep-throated Rex, Gabe still maintained a steady rhythm with a hand fisted around Boone's.

Boone devoured Rex's mouth as he thrust into Gabe's fist, begging for his mouth back. Gabe must have gotten the hint because he pulled off Rex and went back down on Boone. Boone reached over and pinched Rex's sensitive nipple.

"Oh God, sweetheart. I'm gonna come," Rex said as he bit Boone's bottom lip.

Gabe heard the exchange and pulled off Boone. He swallowed Rex down to the root and fingered his hole. As he pushed one finger into Rex's tight puckered hole, Rex shot his cum down Gabe's throat. "Ahh, fuck."

Gabe quickly licked Rex clean then went back to Boone's waiting cock. They could both tell Boone was getting close. Rex knelt beside Gabe and ran his tongue around Boone's now-drawn-up sac. When Rex pushed his tongue against the small divot behind Boone's balls, Boone came with a scream. He yelled out both his lovers' names as his entire body vibrated with his release.

Gabe and Rex took turns licking Boone clean then stood and shared a group kiss. Mixing the flavors of both Rex's and Boone's seed with his two lovers was enough to send Gabe over the edge. Unfortunately he didn't get his jeans down in time and made a mess of himself.

Gabe looked down and rolled his eyes. "Goddammit. I haven't done that since I was in basic training."

Both Rex and Boone looked down at Gabe's now-wet jeans and began to laugh. Rex kissed him on the nose. "I think you look sexy like that, sweetheart."

"Yeah, right. You two just make sure you shield me so I can get back into the house without anyone else seeing." Gabe walked toward the truck and got in. He looked back at Rex and Boone, who were laughing as they walked back to the truck arm in arm.

As they got in the truck, Gabe turned his head toward them and started the truck. "You just wait 'til tonight. I'm gonna make you both scream like girls."

Chapter Fifteen

&

Rex came into the kitchen and took a mug from the cabinet. It had been a week since the last of their free labor had gone back to their homes. He filled his cup with coffee and went to find Maggie.

He found her in the almost-finished rehabilitation center. She smiled as she spotted him coming through the big double doors. "How's my boy today?"

Rex smiled and gave his mom a kiss on the cheek. He handed her his coffee cup and pushed her out the doors and to the big shade tree in the front yard. He sat on a bench beside her and took his mug back.

"It's not a good day, Mom. I just got back from town and it seems not only are Gabe and Boone the talk of Styler but also the rehab center itself." He blew out a breath and took a drink of coffee.

"I overheard the ladies in the bank talking about the perverse relationship going on out at the Double B. Then they had the nerve to say how dare we bring a bunch of cripples into their town without even asking the city council first." Rex knocked his hat off and ran his fingers through his thick hair.

Maggie Cotton narrowed her eyes and looked at her son. "Tell me who was talking about the boys I love."

Rex shrugged his shoulders. "Mrs. Cooper and Mrs. Jennings. If they feel that way, Mom, I bet the whole town does. We can't have disabled people coming into an unfriendly environment."

The small, frail hand of his mom grabbed his. "Look at me, son." When Rex looked into his mom's eyes, she continued. "I've lived in this area all my life and I know for a fact that both of those old busybodies have husbands that have stepped out on them for years. Don't let them get in the way of your happiness. And as for the center…well, you just let me take care of the residents of Styler. You concentrate on the men you love and getting the center up and running. You've got guests already booked for next month."

Rex kissed his mom's cheek. "You always put things in perspective for me, Mom. I love you and I'm glad you're here."

* * * * *

Two weeks later a big story came out in the Oklahoma City newspaper touting the new equestrian rehabilitation center being built just outside Styler. From all the quotes from local townspeople, Rex guessed that they weren't all against it. Of course it was a big coup for the small town of Styler to be recognized by the big Oklahoma City paper. Rex guessed that had a lot more to do with the town's acceptance but he wasn't about to look a gift horse in the mouth. He knew the horse in this case was his own mom.

Sweet little Maggie Cotton had called the newspaper and talked one of the reporters into coming out to the ranch to see what they were doing. Rex remembered being so proud of Boone that day. He talked with passion and brilliance as he showed the reporter what the center would be trying to accomplish. He let her take pictures of the rehabilitation building with all its fancy weight machines and whirlpools and then led her to the barn.

Boone explained the need for the horseback riding therapy the handicapped guests would receive. He showed her the specially designed saddles a local leather craftsman had made and even gave out his name in case anyone would like to purchase one of the saddles from him.

The article was beautiful when it came out. The reporter praised Boone's work and the facility. She even went as far as to interview the two doctors the center had hired. The story had even been picked up by a few national papers. The calls started pouring in asking about treatment reservations and volunteer opportunities. Maggie did her best to try to keep up with the calls but they finally had to hire a woman to answer phones.

Ben had called with the good news that he'd also seen the article in the Santa Fe paper. Gabe told him about the requests coming in for treatment and Ben suggested that they might need to expand the operation in Styler. Maybe even consider talking other benefactors into joining them to open a few more around the country.

* * * * *

Opening day arrived and all the volunteers and paid professionals were in place to welcome their guests. They had a total of twenty people arriving within the next couple of hours, a good mixture of both children and adults.

Boone was so nervous he hadn't slept in two days. Gabe could tell he'd lost weight too. He would have been worried about him but the continuous smile on Boone's face told him they were good nerves not bad.

Gabe thought of the new sign the whole team had helped to put above the ranch entrance. Gabe had been glad to get rid of the Double B sign. The sign was put up and then covered up yesterday by the team. They'd all come in town for the big opening.

Jenny even made it, although the twins were barely three weeks old. Cash and Carson had to be about the cutest little babies he'd ever laid eyes on. Midnight black hair with sweet Jenny's cornflower blue eyes. Cree and Jake were so puffed up with pride, Gabe was surprised they didn't float away on the breeze.

Kate was barely showing but that didn't keep Ben's hand from constantly rubbing her small pregnancy bump. Gabe had never seen his old commanding officer so happy.

Right now, Gabe was on a mission to find Boone and Rex. He'd already looked in the rehab building and the barn but he didn't have any luck. He could think of only one other place they might have snuck off to and that was their bedroom.

Gabe started getting hard just thinking about what they might be doing. He opened the kitchen door and found a sobbing Cory sitting at the kitchen table with a cell phone in her hand.

He quickly sat down next to her and rubbed her back. "What's wrong, Cory? Do you want me to get Remy?"

Cory turned toward Gabe and wrapped her arms around him. She sobbed against his chest as he made gentle shushing noises in her hair. He stroked the long black curls as he spoke softly. "What happened? Did you get a phone call?"

Cory wiped her face with the bottom of her t-shirt. "Someone's trying to drive me crazy. I need you to find Remy and ask him to come in here."

Gabe nodded and pulled out his cell phone. He dialed Remy's cell number. Cory looked at Gabe like she couldn't believe she hadn't thought of calling him.

"Weh," Remy answered his phone.

"Remy, it's Gabe. Cory needs you in the kitchen." He turned away and walked to the screen door. "I think she got a phone call that's upset her. I found her crying at the kitchen table with the phone in her hand."

"Two seconds."

The phone went dead and sure enough about two seconds later Remy came running through the door. He gathered Cory in his arms and carried her to the couch. They were speaking in hushed tones so Gabe assumed it wasn't any of his business and went to find Boone and Rex.

He opened the door of the bedroom and stopped. He expected to find the two men in some crazy sex position but instead he found Boone sound asleep in Rex's arms.

Rex put his finger to his lips. Gabe entered the room and closed the door. He slipped off his boots and stretched out on the other side of Boone.

Rex must've seen the question in his eyes. "Our baby is all worn out. He invited me in for a quick rub-off but by the time I got undressed he was sound asleep. I decided he needed sleep a lot more that I needed to come again so I've just been holding him." Even though Rex was whispering his voice was so deep that it made Gabe's chest rattle. Evidently it made Boone's rattle too because he stirred and snuggled his body even closer to Rex. He pushed his fine ass against Gabe's cock.

Gabe groaned and wrapped his arms around both men. He drew lazy circles on Rex's bare ass. He really wasn't trying to get frisky. He was just overwhelmed with love for these two men.

Rex and Gabe held Boone for the next hour. They didn't speak any more but mouthed words of love every now and then. Rex looked at the clock and motioned to Boone with his eyes. "It's time to wake him up or he's going to miss his own grand opening."

Gabe nodded and they both leaned forward to kiss Boone awake. Gabe whispered in Boone's ear. "Wake up, honey. I know you're still tired but the guests will be here in about twenty minutes."

Boone shot straight up, his eyes trying like hell to open. "Sorry. I-I didn't mean to fall asleep like that."

Rex brushed his hand over Boone's back. "It's perfectly understandable, darlin'. You've nearly killed yourself trying to get everything ready. You've got to make it through another couple hours and then you can sleep."

Rex rose off the bed and went to put fresh clothes on. Gabe followed Rex to the small closet and pulled out a dress-style western shirt with pearl snap buttons. Rex whistled at him when he put it on. "You clean up real nice, sweetheart."

Gabe smacked his ass and reached for a clean pair of jeans. "Don't get used to it, baby. I'm a t-shirt kinda guy."

Boone joined them and leaned in to give Gabe a kiss. "You're our kinda guy." He turned and kissed Rex. "Thank you both…for everything."

They finished dressing in between soft playful kisses. They made it outside just in time to see the first few cars pull into the nicely paved ranch yard. Gabe looked over at the main house. It was still under construction but at least the outside was complete. He looked around the ranch and smiled. They'd done a damn good thing here.

Volunteers had poured in from the town in the last couple of weeks. They'd planted flowers in every bit of soil that wasn't paved and put whiskey barrels full of flowers where it was paved.

Gabe and Rex followed Boone as he welcomed the arriving guests. When it looked like everyone had arrived they led the group of friends and guests to the new sign.

Gabe and Rex took Boone's hands and stood in front of the large timber sign. Gabe turned to Boone. "You know we've talked a lot about renaming the Double B. Well, Rex and I finally decided that the whole ranch should bear the foundation's name and the team helped us get this sign." He motioned to Mac and Nicco, who had their hands on the ropes tied to each end of the king-size sheet that covered the sign. On Gabe's nod the men pulled the ropes and the sheet fluttered to the ground.

Boone looked up at the sign and closed his eyes. He squatted down and breathed deeply like he was about to pass out. Rex and Gabe knelt on either side of him.

Gabe ran his fingers through Boone's long blond hair. "You've brought his dream and yours to life, honey. Stand up and look at your sign. You deserve this moment."

Boone nodded and rose. He wiped the tears from his eyes and looked at the large sign. The Timothy Fowler Riding Center. Boone wiped a few more tears and looked at the friends and guests surrounding him. He filled the guests in on who Timothy Fowler was and why he'd always dreamed of working in a facility such as the one in front of him.

When he was finished the staff handed out plastic wineglasses to everyone. The glasses were filled with sparkling cider to toast the opening of the center. Boone raised his glass toward the sign. "For you, Tim. I love you, brother."

Also by Carol Lynne

ഩ

eBooks:

Feels So Right

Finnegan's Promise

Gio's Dream

Harvest Heat

Men in Love 1: Branded by Gold

Men in Love 2: Ben's Wildflower

Men in Love 3: Open to Possibilities

Men in Love 4: Completing the Circle

Men in Love 5: Going Against Orders

Men in Love 6: Tortured Souls

Necklace of Shame

Never Too Old

No Longer His

Riding the Wolf

Saddle Up and Ride 1: Reining in the Past

Saddle Up and Ride 2: Bareback Cowboy

Sex With Lex

Sunshine, Sex and Sunflowers

Print Books:

Branded by Love *(anthology)*

Down Under Temptation *(anthology)*

Forbidden Love *(anthology)*

Protected Love *(anthology)*

Naughtiest Nuptials *(anthology)*

Taboo Treats *(anthology)*

About the Author

ꟷ

I've been a reading fanatic for years and finally at the age of 40 decided to try my hand at writing. I've always loved romance novels that are just a little bit naughty so naturally my books tend to go just a little further. It's my fantasy world after all.

When I'm not being a mother to a five-year-old and a six-year-old, you can usually find me in my deep leather chair with either a book in my hand or my laptop.

ꟷ

The author welcomes comments from readers. You can find her website and email address on her author bio page at www.ellorascave.com.

Tell Us What You Think

We appreciate hearing reader opinions about our books. You can email us at Comments@EllorasCave.com.

Why an electronic book?

We live in the Information Age—an exciting time in the history of human civilization, in which technology rules supreme and continues to progress in leaps and bounds every minute of every day. For a multitude of reasons, more and more avid literary fans are opting to purchase e-books instead of paper books. The question from those not yet initiated into the world of electronic reading is simply: *Why?*

1. ***Price.*** An electronic title at Ellora's Cave Publishing and Cerridwen Press runs anywhere from 40% to 75% less than the cover price of the exact same title in paperback format. Why? Basic mathematics and cost. It is less expensive to publish an e-book (no paper and printing, no warehousing and shipping) than it is to publish a paperback, so the savings are passed along to the consumer.
2. ***Space.*** Running out of room in your house for your books? That is one worry you will never have with electronic books. For a low one-time cost, you can purchase a handheld device specifically designed for e-reading. Many e-readers have large, convenient screens for viewing. Better yet, hundreds of titles can be stored within your new library—on a single microchip. There are a variety of e-readers from different manufacturers. You can also read e-books on your PC or laptop computer. (Please note that Ellora's Cave does not endorse any specific brands.

You can check our websites at www.ellorascave.com or www.cerridwenpress.com for information we make available to new consumers.)

3. ***Mobility.*** Because your new e-library consists of only a microchip within a small, easily transportable e-reader, your entire cache of books can be taken with you wherever you go.
4. ***Personal Viewing Preferences.*** Are the words you are currently reading too small? Too large? Too... ANNOYING? Paperback books cannot be modified according to personal preferences, but e-books can.
5. ***Instant Gratification.*** Is it the middle of the night and all the bookstores near you are closed? Are you tired of waiting days, sometimes weeks, for bookstores to ship the novels you bought? Ellora's Cave Publishing sells instantaneous downloads twenty-four hours a day, seven days a week, every day of the year. Our webstore is never closed. Our e-book delivery system is 100% automated, meaning your order is filled as soon as you pay for it.

Those are a few of the top reasons why electronic books are replacing paperbacks for many avid readers.

As always, Ellora's Cave and Cerridwen Press welcome your questions and comments. We invite you to email us at Comments@ellorascave.com or write to us directly at Ellora's Cave Publishing Inc., 1056 Home Avenue, Akron, OH 44310-3502.

ELLORA'S CAVE
ROMANTICA PUBLISHING

CPSIA information can be obtained at www.ICGtesting.com
232911LV00001B/199/P

9 781419 964275